ATTACK OF THE JACK-O'-LANTERNS

GOOSEBUMPS®
MOST WANTED

#1 PLANET OF THE LAWN GNOMES
#2 SON OF SLAPPY
#3 HOW I MET MY MONSTER
#4 FRANKENSTEIN'S DOG
#5 DR. MANIAC WILL SEE YOU NOW
#6 CREATURE TEACHER: FINAL EXAM
#7 A NIGHTMARE ON CLOWN STREET
#8 NIGHT OF THE PUPPET PEOPLE
#9 HERE COMES THE SHAGGEDY
#10 THE LIZARD OF OZ

SPECIAL EDITION #1 ZOMBIE HALLOWEEN
SPECIAL EDITION #2 THE 12 SCREAMS OF CHRISTMAS
SPECIAL EDITION #3 TRICK OR TRAP
SPECIAL EDITION #4 THE HAUNTER

GOOSEBUMPS®
SLAPPYWORLD

#1 SLAPPY BIRTHDAY TO YOU
#2 ATTACK OF THE JACK
#3 I AM SLAPPY'S EVIL TWIN
#4 PLEASE DO NOT FEED THE WEIRDO
#5 ESCAPE FROM SHUDDER MANSION

GOOSEBUMPS®

Also available as ebooks

NIGHT OF THE LIVING DUMMY
DEEP TROUBLE
MONSTER BLOOD
THE HAUNTED MASK

ONE DAY AT HORRORLAND
THE CURSE OF THE MUMMY'S TOMB
BE CAREFUL WHAT YOU WISH FOR
SAY CHEESE AND DIE!
THE HORROR AT CAMP JELLYJAM
HOW I GOT MY SHRUNKEN HEAD
THE WEREWOLF OF FEVER SWAMP
A NIGHT IN TERROR TOWER
WELCOME TO DEAD HOUSE
WELCOME TO CAMP NIGHTMARE
GHOST BEACH
THE SCARECROW WALKS AT MIDNIGHT
YOU CAN'T SCARE ME!
RETURN OF THE MUMMY
REVENGE OF THE LAWN GNOMES
PHANTOM OF THE AUDITORIUM
VAMPIRE BREATH
STAY OUT OF THE BASEMENT
A SHOCKER ON SHOCK STREET
LET'S GET INVISIBLE!
NIGHT OF THE LIVING DUMMY 2
NIGHT OF THE LIVING DUMMY 3
THE ABOMINABLE SNOWMAN OF PASADENA
THE BLOB THAT ATE EVERYONE
THE GHOST NEXT DOOR
THE HAUNTED CAR
ATTACK OF THE GRAVEYARD GHOULS
PLEASE DON'T FEED THE VAMPIRE!
THE HEADLESS GHOST
THE HAUNTED MASK 2
BRIDE OF THE LIVING DUMMY
ATTACK OF THE JACK-O'-LANTERNS

ALSO AVAILABLE:

IT CAME FROM OHIO!: MY LIFE AS A WRITER by R.L. Stine

R.L. STINE

SCHOLASTIC INC.

Goosebumps book series created by Parachute Press, Inc.

ISBN 978-1-338-31868-5

12 11 10 9 8 7 6 5 4 3 2 1 18 19 20 21 22

Printed in the U.S.A. 40

First printing, August 2018

1

"Where are you going, Elf?" Dad called from the den.

"Don't call me Elf!" I shouted back. "My name is Drew."

Dad thinks it's real cute to call me Elf, but I hate it. He calls me Elf because I'm tiny for a twelve-year-old. And I have short, straight black hair and sort of a pointy chin and a pointy little nose.

If you looked like an elf, would you want people calling you Elf?

Of course not.

One day my best friend, Walker Parkes, heard my dad call me Elf. So Walker tried it. "What's up, Elf?" Walker said.

I stomped on Walker's foot as hard as I could, and he never called me that again.

"Where are you going, *Drew*?" Dad called from the den.

"Out," I told him, and slammed the front door behind me. I like to keep my parents guessing. I try never to give them a straight answer.

You might say I'm as mischievous as an elf. But if you said it, I'd stomp on *your* foot, too!

I'm tough. Ask anyone. They'll tell you that Drew Brockman is tough. When you're the shrimpiest girl in your class, you've *got* to be tough.

Actually, I wasn't going anywhere. I was waiting for my friends to come to my house. I walked down to the street to watch for them.

I took a deep breath. The people in the corner house had a fire going in their fireplace. The white smoke floated out from their chimney. It smelled so sweet and piney.

I love autumn. It means Halloween is on the way.

Halloween is my favorite holiday. I guess I like it so much because it gives me a chance to look like someone else. Or some*thing* else.

It's the one night of the year that I don't have to look like pointy-chinned me.

But I have a problem with Halloween. Two kids in my class are the problem. Tabitha Weiss and Lee Winston.

For the past two years, Tabby and Lee have totally *ruined* Halloween for Walker and me.

I'm so angry about it. Walker is angry, too. Our favorite holiday *ruined* because of two stuck-up kids who think they can do whatever they want.

Grrrrrrr.

Just thinking about it makes me want to punch someone!

My other friends, Shane and Shana Martin, are upset about it, too. Shane and Shana are brother and sister, twins my age. They live in the house next door, and we hang out a lot.

Shane and Shana don't look like anyone else I know. They both have very round faces with curly ringlets of blond hair. They have red cheeks and cheery smiles, and they're both short and kind of chunky.

The twins are as angry as Walker and me about Tabby and Lee. And *this* Halloween, we're going to do something about it.

Only we don't know what we're going to do.

That's why they're coming over to my house to discuss it.

How did the Tabby and Lee problem start? Well, I have to go back two years to explain it to you.

I remember it so clearly.

Walker and I were ten. We were just hanging out in front of my house. Walker had his bike on its side and was doing something to the spokes on one wheel.

It was a beautiful autumn day. Down the block, someone was burning a big pile of leaves. It's against the law here in Riverdale. My dad always threatens to call the police when someone burns leaves. But I love the smell.

Walker was fiddling with his bike, and I was watching him. I forget what we were talking about. I glanced up—and there stood Tabby and Lee.

Tabby looked as perfect as always. "Little Miss Perfect." That's what Dad calls her—and for once, he's right.

The wind was blowing pretty hard. But her long, straight blond hair stayed in place. It didn't fly out all over her head like mine did.

Tabby has perfect creamy-white skin and perfect green eyes that sparkle a lot. She's very pretty, and she knows it.

Sometimes it takes all my strength not to shake both hands in her hair and mess it all up!

Lee is tall and good-looking, with brown skin, dark brown eyes and a great, warm smile. He sort of struts when he walks and acts real cool.

The girls at school all think he's terrific. But I can never understand a word he says. That's because he always has a huge wad of green-apple bubble gum in his mouth.

"Mmmmmbbb mmmmbbbbb." Lee stared down at Walker's bike and mumbled something.

"Hey," I said. "What's up, guys?"

Tabby made a disgusted face and pointed a finger at me. "Drew, you have something hanging from your nose," she said.

"Oh!" I shot my hand up and rubbed the bottom of my nose. Nothing there.

"Sorry," Tabby snickered. "It only looked like you did."

Tabby and Lee both laughed.

Tabby is always playing mean jokes like that on me. She knows I'm self-conscious about how I look. So I always fall for her dumb tricks.

"Nice bike," Lee mumbled to Walker. "How many speeds?"

"It's a twelve-speed," Walker told him.

Lee sneered. "Mine is a forty-two-speed."

"Huh?" Walker jumped to his feet. "There's no such thing as a forty-two-speed!" he cried.

"Mine is," Lee insisted, still sneering. "It's specially made."

He blew a big green bubble-gum bubble. That's hard to do while you're sneering.

I wanted to pop it all over his smug face. But he stepped back and popped it himself.

"Did you get a haircut?" Tabby asked me, studying my windblown hair.

"No," I replied.

"I didn't think so," she said. She smoothed her perfect hair back with one hand.

"Grrrrrrr." I couldn't help it. I balled my hands into fists and let out an angry growl.

I growl a lot. Sometimes I don't even know I'm doing it.

"Mummmmmbb mmmmbbbbb." Lee said something. Bubble-gum juice ran down his chin.

"Excuse me?" I asked.

"I'm having a Halloween party," he repeated.

My heart started to pound. "A real Halloween party?" I demanded. "With everyone in costumes, and hot apple cider, and games and bobbing for apples, and scary stories?"

Lee nodded. "Yes. A real Halloween party. At my house on Halloween night. You guys want to come?"

"Sure!" Walker and I replied.

Big mistake. *Real* big mistake.

The Halloween party was already crowded with kids from school when Walker and I showed up. Lee's parents had orange and black streamers strung up all over the living room. Three huge jack-o'-lanterns grinned at us from the window seat by the front window.

Of course Tabby was the first person I ran into. Even in costume, she wasn't hard to recognize. She was dressed as a princess.

Perfect?

She wore a frilly pink princess-type gown with long, puffy sleeves and a high, lacy collar. And she had her blond hair pinned up with a sparkly rhinestone tiara in it.

She smiled her lipsticked lips at me. "Is that you, Drew?" she asked, pretending she didn't recognize me. "What are you supposed to be? A mouse?"

"No!" I protested. "I'm not a mouse. I'm a Klingon. Don't you ever watch *Star Trek*?"

Tabby snickered. "Are you *sure* you're not a mouse?"

She turned and walked away. She had a pleased smile on her face. She gets such a thrill from insulting me.

I growled under my breath and searched for someone else to talk to. I found Shane and Shana in front of the fireplace. The twins were easy to recognize. They were both big, puffy white snowmen.

"Excellent costumes!" I greeted them.

They wore two white snowballs. One big snowball over their bodies. A smaller snowball over their heads.

The snowman faces had eyeholes cut in them. But I couldn't tell Shane from Shana. "What is the snow made of?" I asked.

"Styrofoam," Shana answered. She has a high, squeaky voice. So now I knew who was who. "We carved them out of big blocks of it."

"Cool," I said.

"Great party, huh?" Shane chimed in. "Everyone from our class is here. Did you see Bryna Morse's costume? She sprayed her whole body with silver spray paint. Her face and hair, too!"

"What's she supposed to be?" I demanded, searching the crowded room for her. "Silver Surfer?"

"No. I think the Statue of Liberty," Shane replied. "She was carrying a plastic torch."

A loud crackle in the fireplace made me jump. Most of the lights were off, giving the room a dark, Halloween mood. The fire made long shadows dance over the floor.

I turned and saw Walker making his way to us. His entire body was wrapped in bandages and gauze. He was a mummy.

"I'm in trouble," he announced.

"What's your problem?" Shane asked.

"My mom did a terrible wrapping job," Walker complained. "I'm coming unraveled." He struggled to retie the loose bandages around his neck.

"Aaaagh!" He let out an angry cry. "The whole thing is coming undone!"

"Are you wearing clothes underneath?" Shana asked.

Shane and I laughed. I pictured Walker huddled in the middle of the party in his underwear, piles of bandages at his feet.

"Yes. I've got my clothes on underneath the costume," Walker replied. "But if these bandages all come undone, I'll fall on my face!"

"Hey—what's up?" Lee interrupted. He wore a Batman costume, but I recognized his dark eyes under the mask. And I recognized his voice.

"Awesome party," Shana said.

"Yeah. Awesome," I repeated.

Lee started to reply. But a thunderous *crash* made everyone gasp.

We all froze. "What was *that*?" Lee cried.

The crowded room grew silent.

I heard another crash. Bumping sounds. Low voices.

"It—it's coming from the basement!" Lee stammered. He pulled off the Batman mask. His bushy hair fell over his face, but I could see his frightened expression.

We all turned to the open doorway at the far end of the living room. Beyond the doorway, stairs led down to Lee's basement.

"Oh!" Lee gasped as we heard another crash.

Then heavy footsteps—up the basement stairs.

"Someone is in the house!" Lee shrieked in terror. "Someone has broken in!"

"Mom! Dad!" Lee cried. His voice rang out shrilly in the silent living room. The rest of us had all frozen in place.

A shiver ran down my back as I listened to the heavy footsteps treading up the stairs.

"Mom! Dad! Help!" Lee called again, his eyes bulging with fear.

No reply.

He took off toward their bedroom at the back of the house. "Mom? Dad?"

I started to run after him. But he returned to the living room a few seconds later, his whole body trembling. "My parents—they're *gone*!"

"Call the police!" someone shouted.

"Yes! Call nine-one-one!" Walker screamed.

Lee hurtled to the phone beside the couch. His foot kicked over a can of Pepsi on the rug. But he didn't notice.

He grabbed the phone receiver and jammed it to his ear. I saw him push the emergency number.

But then he turned to us and let the phone fall from his hand. "It's dead. The line is dead!"

Some kids gasped. A few cried out.

I turned to Walker and opened my mouth to speak. But before I could get a sound out, two bulky figures burst out from the basement doorway.

"Noooooo!" Lee let out a horrified howl. Tabby stepped up and huddled close beside him. Her heavily made-up eyes were wide with fright. She grabbed Lee's arm.

The two intruders moved quickly into the living-room entrance and blocked the doorway. One of them had a blue wool ski mask pulled down over his face. The other wore a rubber gorilla mask.

They both wore black leather jackets over black jeans.

"Party time!" the gorilla shouted in a gruff voice. He laughed. A cruel laugh. "Party time, everyone!"

Several kids cried out. My heart started to pound in my chest. I suddenly felt hot and cold at the same time.

"Who are you?" Lee demanded over the frightened cries of some kids. "How did you get in? Where are my parents?"

"Parents?" the guy in the ski mask replied. He had bright blue eyes, almost as blue as the wool mask that covered his face. "Do you have parents?"

They both laughed.

"Where are they?" Lee cried.

"I think they ran away when they saw us coming!" the guy said through the ski mask.

Lee swallowed hard. A tiny gulping sound escaped his throat.

Tabby stepped in front of him. "You can't come in here!" she shouted angrily to the two intruders. "We're having a party!"

The gorilla turned to his partner and laughed. They both laughed loudly, tossing back their heads.

"It's *our* party now!" the gorilla announced. "We're taking over!"

Hushed gasps rang out around the room. My legs suddenly felt rubbery and weak. I grabbed Walker's shoulder to keep from collapsing.

"Wh-what are you going to do?" Tabby demanded.

"Everybody down on the floor!" the guy in the ski mask ordered.

"You can't do this!" Tabby screamed.

"We're just kids!" someone else cried. "Are you going to rob us? We don't have any money!"

I saw Shane and Shana huddled together by the fireplace. Their faces were hidden by their snowman costumes. But I knew they must be terrified, too.

"*Down on the floor!*" both intruders screamed.

The room echoed with heavy thuds and the rustle of costumes as we all obediently dropped to the floor.

"You, too!" the gorilla screamed at Shane and Shana.

"It's impossible! How can we get down in these big snowballs?" Shana cried.

"Get down on the floor anyway," the gorilla ordered nastily.

"Get down—or we'll push you down," the ski-masked guy threatened.

I watched Shane and Shana struggle to lower themselves to the floor. They had to pull off their bottom snowballs to get onto their knees. Shana's snowball broke in half as she worked to pull it off.

"Okay—push-ups, everybody!" the gorilla ordered.

"Huh?" Confused cries rose up through the room.

"Push-ups!" the gorilla repeated. "You all know how to do push-ups—right?"

"How—how many do we have to do?" Walker asked. He knelt close beside me on the rug in front of the coffee table.

"Do them for a couple of hours," the ski-masked guy replied.

"Hours?" several kids cried out.

"A few hours of push-ups will get you all warmed up," the gorilla said. "Then we'll think of something harder for you to do!"

"Yeah. *Much* harder!" his partner added. Then they both burst out laughing again.

"You can't do this!" I screamed. My voice came out high and tiny, like a mouse voice.

Other kids protested, too. I turned to the door. The guy in the ski mask had moved into the living room. But the gorilla was still blocking any escape.

"Get started!" the gorilla ordered.

"Or we'll make it *three* hours!" his partner added.

I heard a lot of groans and complaints. But we all dropped onto our stomachs and started doing push-ups.

What choice did we have?

"We can't do this for two hours!" Walker protested breathlessly. "We'll *faint*!"

He raised and dropped, raised and dropped, close beside me on the floor. His mummy costume was unraveling with each move he made.

"Faster!" the gorilla ordered. "Come on. Speed it up!"

I had done only four or five push-ups, and my arms already started to ache. There was no way I'd last for more than ten or fifteen minutes.

I raised my eyes to the front of the room—and saw a sight that made me cry out in shock.

5

"Walker—look!" I whispered.

"Hunnh?" he groaned.

I poked Walker in the side.

He lost his balance and hit the floor. "Hey, Drew! What's your problem?" he groaned.

We both turned our eyes to the doorway.

And saw to our surprise that Tabby and Lee weren't down on the floor with the rest of us. They had joined the two intruders in front of the doorway.

And they both had wide, gleeful grins on their faces.

I stopped the push-ups and raised myself to my knees. I saw Lee start to laugh.

Tabby joined him. She laughed so hard, her tiara shook. They slapped each other a high five.

All around me on the floor, some kids were still working away, pushing themselves up, then down, up, then down. Groaning and grunting as they obediently did their push-ups.

But Walker and I had stopped. We were both on our knees, watching Tabby and Lee. The two creeps were laughing and celebrating.

I was about to cry out in anger—when the two intruders tugged off their masks.

I instantly recognized the boy with the gorilla mask. He was Todd Jeffrey, a high-school kid who lives next door to Lee.

I knew the ski-mask kid, too. His name was Joe Something-or-other. He is a friend of Todd's.

Todd brushed his coppery hair back off his forehead. His hair was wet, his face was red, and he was sweating. I guess it was hot inside that rubber mask.

Joe tossed his ski mask to the floor. He shook his head, laughing at us. "All a joke, guys!" he called out. "Happy Halloween!"

All the other kids had stopped the push-ups. But no one had moved from the floor. I guess we were too shocked to stand up.

"Just a party joke!" Lee chimed in, grinning.

"Did we scare you?" Tabby asked coyly.

"Grrrrrr!" I let out the loudest growl I ever growled. I wanted to leap up, grab the tiara off Princess Tabby's head, and wrap it around her neck!

Todd and Joe slapped each other a high five. They picked up cans of Pepsi and tilted them up over their mouths.

"You can get up now!" Lee announced, snickering.

"Wow! You guys looked so *scared*!" Tabby cried gleefully. "I guess we really fooled you!"

"I don't believe this," Walker muttered, shaking his head. The wrapping had fallen from his face. Bandages drooped loosely over his shoulders. "I really don't believe this. What a mean, rotten joke."

I climbed up shakily and helped Walker to his feet. I heard Shane and Shana grumbling behind us. Their costumes were totally wrecked.

Kids were grumbling and complaining. Tabby and Lee were the only ones laughing. No one else thought the joke was the least bit funny.

I started across the room to tell the two creeps what I thought of their dumb joke. But Lee's parents burst into the room, pulling off their coats.

"We went next door to the Jeffreys'," Lee's mom announced. Then she saw Todd. "Oh, hi, Todd. We were just at your house, visiting your parents. What are you doing over here? Helping Lee out with the party?"

"Kind of," Todd replied, grinning.

"How's the party going?" Lee's dad asked.

"Great," Lee told him. "Just great, Dad."

And that's how Tabby and Lee ruined Halloween two years ago.

Walker and I—and Shane and Shana, too—were all really upset.

No. We were more than upset. We were furious.

Halloween is our favorite holiday. And we don't like to see it ruined because of a mean practical joke.

So, last year we decided to get even.

"We need special decorations," Shana said. "Not the same old pumpkins and skeletons."

"Yeah. Something scarier," Shane chimed in.

"I think jack-o'-lanterns are plenty scary," I insisted. "Especially when you put candles in them. And their dark faces light up with those jagged, evil grins."

"Jack-o'-lanterns are babyish," Walker argued. "No one is afraid of a jack-o'-lantern. Shana is right. If we're going to scare Tabby and Lee, we need something better."

It was a week before Halloween. The four of us were hard at work at my house. We were working on *my* Halloween party.

Yes. Last year, the party was at my house.

Why did I decide to have the party? For only one reason.

For revenge.

For revenge on Tabby and Lee.

Walker, Shane, Shana, and I had spent the entire year talking about it, dreaming up plans. Dreaming up the most frightening scares we could imagine.

We didn't want to pull a mean joke like having people break into the house.

That was *too* mean. And too frightening.

Some of my friends *still* have bad dreams about guys in ski masks and gorilla masks.

The four of us didn't want to terrify *all* of our guests. We just wanted to embarrass Tabby and Lee—and scare them out of their skins!

Now, a week before the big night, we were sitting around my living room after dinner. We should have been doing homework. But Halloween was too near.

We had no time for homework. We had to spend all of our time making evil plans.

Shane and Shana had a lot of really frightening ideas. They both look so sweet and innocent. But once you get to know them, they're pretty weird.

Walker and I wanted to keep our scares simple. The simpler, the scarier. That's what we thought.

I wanted to drop fake cobwebs over Tabby and Lee from the stairway. I know a store that sells really sticky, scratchy cobwebs.

Walker has a tarantula that he keeps in a glass cage in his room. A live tarantula. He thought maybe we could tangle the tarantula in the cobwebs and then drop it in Tabby's hair.

Not a bad idea.

Walker also wanted to cut a trapdoor in the living-room floor. When Tabby and Lee stepped on the spot, we'd open the trapdoor, and they would disappear into the basement.

I had to reject that idea. I liked it. But I wasn't sure how Mom and Dad would react when they discovered us sawing up the floor.

Also, I just wanted to terrify the two creeps. I didn't want to break their necks.

"Where are we going to put the fake blood puddles?" Shane asked.

He held a red plastic puddle of blood in each hand. He and his sister had bought a dozen fake blood puddles at a costume store. They came in different sizes, and looked very real.

"And don't forget the green slime," Shana reminded us. She had three plastic bags of slime beside her.

Walker and I opened one of the bags and felt the slimy, sticky, oozy gunk. "Where did you buy this?" I asked. "At the same store?"

"No. It came out of Shana's nose!" Shane joked.

With an angry cry, Shana hoisted up one of the bags. She swung it in front of her, threatening to smack her brother with it.

He laughed and bounced off the couch.

"Whoa! Careful!" I cried. "If that bag breaks—"

"Maybe we can hang the slime from the ceiling," Walker suggested.

"Yeah! Cool!" Shane cried excitedly. "And it could drip down onto Tabby and Lee."

"Maybe we could cover them in it!" Walker added excitedly. "And they'd look like two sticky, green blobs."

"Glub glub glub!" Shana thrashed out her arms and pretended she was drowning under a puddle of slime.

"Will it stick to the ceiling?" I asked. "How will we keep it up there long enough? How will we get the two of them to stand under it?"

I'm the practical one in the group. They have a lot of wild ideas. But they never know how to make them work.

That's my job.

"I'm not sure," Walker replied. He jumped up from his chair. "I'm going to get something to drink."

"What if the slime started to spew out of the jack-o'-lanterns?" Shane suggested. "That would be kind of scary—wouldn't it?"

"What if we had fake blood gush out of the jack-o'-lanterns?" Shana said. "That would be even scarier."

"We have to trap Tabby and Lee somehow," Shane suggested, thinking hard. "All this slime and cobwebs and blood is good. But we have to make them think they're really in danger. We have to make them think that something *terrible* is really going to happen to them."

I started to agree — but the lights went out.

"Oh!" I uttered a cry of surprise, blinking in the sudden darkness. "What happened?"

Shane and Shana didn't reply.

The curtains were drawn. So no light entered the living room from outside. The room was so dark, I couldn't see my two friends sitting right across from me!

And then, I heard a dry, whispered voice. A frightening whisper, so close, so close to my ear:

"Come with me.
Come home with me now.
Come home to where you belong.
Come home — to the grave."

7

Staring into the darkness, the whispered words sent a shiver down my back.

"Come with me.
Come home with me now.
Come home to where you belong.
Come to your grave, Tabby and Lee.
I have come for you and you alone.
Come, Tabby and Lee. Come with me now."

"That's excellent!" I cried.

The lights flashed back on. Across from me, Shane and Shana clapped and cheered.

"Good job, Walker!" I turned to congratulate him.

He set a recorder on the coffee table in front of us. "I think it will scare them," he said.

"It scared *me*!" I told him. "And I knew what it was."

"When the lights go out and that voice starts to whisper, it will creep *everyone* out!" Shana exclaimed. "Especially with it playing from right under the couch."

"Who recorded the voice?" Shane asked Walker. "Did you do it?"

Walker nodded.

"Cool," Shane said. He turned to me. "But, Drew, I still think you should let Shana and me do some of *our* scares on Tabby and Lee."

"Let's save those for when we really need them," I replied.

I bent down and opened one of the plastic bags. I dug a hand in and pulled out a big chunk of green slime. It felt cold and gooey in my hand.

I worked it around in my palm, squeezing it and shaping it. Then I rolled it into a ball.

"Think it's sticky enough to hang from the ceiling?" I asked. "It would be a nice effect to have it running down the walls. I think—"

"No. I've got a better idea," Walker interrupted. "The lights all go out—right? And the creepy voice starts to whisper. And when it whispers their names—when it whispers, 'Come to your grave, Tabby and Lee'—then someone sneaks up behind each of them and drops a huge glob of slime on their heads."

"That's cool!" Shane declared. We all laughed and cheered.

We had some good ideas. But we needed more. I didn't want to slip up. I didn't want Tabby and Lee to think it was funny, all a big joke.

I wanted them to be SCARED—with a capital S-C-A-R-E-D.

So we thought of more scary ideas. And more ideas.

We worked all week. From after school until late at night. Setting traps. Hiding little creepy surprises all over the living room.

We carved the ugliest jack-o'-lanterns you ever saw. And we filled them with real-looking plastic cockroaches.

We made an eight-foot-tall, papier-mâché monster. And we rigged it to fall out of the coat closet when we pulled a string.

We bought real-looking rubber snakes and worms and spiders and hid them all around the house.

We didn't eat or sleep. We dragged ourselves through school, thinking only about more ways to terrify our two special guests.

Finally, Halloween arrived.

The four of us gathered at my house. We were too tense to sit still or even stand still. We moved around the house, barely speaking to each other. And we carefully checked and rechecked all of the frightening traps and tricks we had prepared.

I had never worked so hard in all my life. Never!

I spent so much time getting ready for the party—and our revenge—that I didn't even think of my Halloween costume until the very last minute.

And so I ended up wearing the same Klingon costume I had worn the year before.

Walker was a pirate that year. He had a patch over one eye and wore a striped shirt and a parrot on one shoulder.

Shane and Shana had dressed as some kind of creatures. I couldn't really tell *what* they were supposed to be.

We didn't care about our costumes. We only cared about scaring Tabby and Lee.

And then, as we paced the living room nervously, one hour before the party was to start, the phone rang.

And we received a call that filled us all with horror.

I was standing right next to the phone when it rang. The harsh buzz nearly made me jump out of my skin. Was I a little tense? YES!

I grabbed the phone in the middle of the first ring. "Hello?"

I heard a familiar voice on the other end. "Hi, Drew. It's Tabby."

"Tabby!" I cried. I decided she was calling to find out what time the party started. "The party starts at eight," I said. "But if you and Lee—"

"That's why I'm calling," Tabby interrupted. "Lee and I can't come tonight."

"Huh?"

The phone dropped out of my hand. It clattered to the floor.

I dove to pick up the receiver, stumbled, and nearly knocked the whole table over.

"What? What did you say?" I demanded.

"Lee and I can't come." Tabby repeated the chilling words. "We're going to Lee's cousin's instead. His cousin gets to trick-or-treat until midnight. He does four different neighborhoods. He promised we'll get bags and bags of candy. Sorry."

"But, Tabby—" I started to protest weakly.

"Sorry," she said. "See you. Bye."

She hung up.

I let out a hoarse wail and sank to my knees on the floor.

"What's wrong?" Walker demanded.

"They—they—they—" I couldn't get the words out.

My three friends huddled around me. Walker tried to pull me to my feet. But my head was spinning. I didn't want to stand up.

"They're *not coming*!" I finally managed to choke out. "Not coming."

"Oh," Walker replied softly. Shane and Shana shook their heads glumly, but didn't say a word.

We all stayed frozen in place, stunned, too miserable to talk. Thinking about all the work . . . all the planning and all the hard work.

A *whole year* of planning and work.

I'm not going to cry, I told myself. I feel like crying, but I'm not going to.

I climbed shakily to my feet. And glanced at the couch.

"What is *that*?" I shrieked.

Everyone turned and saw what I saw. A huge, ugly hole in one of the brown leather couch cushions.

"Oh, no!" Shana wailed. "I was playing with a ball of green slime. I must have dropped it onto the couch when I stood up. It—it *burned a hole* in the cushion!"

"Quick—cover it up before Mom and Dad see—" I started.

Of course Mom and Dad came strolling into the living room. "How's it going?" Dad asked. "All ready for your guests?"

I crossed my fingers and prayed they wouldn't see the huge hole in the couch.

"Good heavens! What happened to the couch?" Mom shrieked.

It took Mom and Dad a long time to get over the ruined couch.

And it took me even longer to get over the ruined party.

That's how it went *last* Halloween. Two years. Two years of ruined Halloweens.

Now it's a year later.

Halloween time again. This year, we have *twice* as much reason to get revenge on Tabby and Lee.

If only we had a plan . . .

9

"This year I'm a space princess," Tabby announced.

She had her blond hair piled high once again, with the same rhinestone tiara in it. And she wore the same long, lacy dress.

The same costume as two years ago. But to add the outer-space look, Tabby had painted her face bright green.

She always has to be a princess, I thought bitterly. *Green or not green, she's still a princess.*

Lee showed up in a cape and tights and said he was Superman. He said it was his little brother's costume. He told us why he didn't have time to get a costume of his own. But I couldn't understand him because of the big wad of bubble gum in his mouth.

Walker and I had decided to be ghosts. We cut eyeholes in bedsheets, and armholes, and that was that.

My sheet dragged behind me on the grass. I should have cut it shorter. But it was too late. We were already on our way to trick-or-treat.

"Where are Shane and Shana?" Lee asked.

"I guess we'll catch up with them," I replied. I raised my trick-or-treat bag in front of me. "Let's get going."

The four of us stepped out into a clear, cold night. A pale half-moon floated low over the houses. The grass shone gray under a light blanket of frost.

We stopped at the bottom of my driveway. A minivan rumbled by. I saw two big dogs peering out the back window. The driver slowed to stare at us as she passed by.

"Where shall we start?" Tabby asked.

Lee mumbled something I didn't understand.

"I want to trick-or-treat all night!" Walker exclaimed. "This may be our last trick-or-treat night ever."

"Excuse me? What do you mean?" Tabby demanded, turning her green face to him.

"Next year, we'll be teenagers," Walker explained. "We'll be too old to trick-or-treat."

Kind of a sad thought.

I tried to take a deep breath of cool air. But I had forgotten to cut a nose or mouth hole in the sheet. We hadn't even left my front yard, and I was already starting to feel hot!

"Let's start at The Willows," I suggested.

The Willows is a neighborhood of small houses. It starts on the other side of a small woods, just two blocks away.

"Why The Willows?" Tabby demanded, fiddling with her tiara.

"Because the houses are real close together," I told her. "We won't have to walk much, and we'll get a lot of candy. No long driveways to walk up and down."

"Sounds good," Lee agreed.

We started walking along the curb. Across the street, I saw two monsters and a skeleton making their way across a front yard. Little kids, followed by a father.

The wind fluttered my costume as we walked. My shoes crunched over frost-covered dead leaves. The sky seemed to grow darker as we made our way past the bare black trees of the woods.

A few minutes later, we reached the first block of The Willows. Streetlights cast a warm yellow glow over the neighborhood. A lot of the houses were decorated with orange and green lights, cutouts of witches and goblins, and flickering jack-o'-lanterns.

The four of us began walking from house to house, gleefully yelling "Trick or treat!" and collecting all kinds of candy.

People oohed and aahed over Tabby's princess costume. She was the only one in our group who had bothered to put on a decent costume. So I guess she stood out.

We passed by a lot of other kids as we made our way down the block. Most of them appeared younger than us. One kid was dressed as a milk carton. He even had all the nutritional information printed on one side.

It took us about half an hour to do both sides of the street. The Willows ended in a cul-de-sac. Kind of a dead end.

"Where to next?" Tabby asked.

"Whoa. Wait. One more house," Walker said. He pointed to a small brick house set back in the trees.

"I didn't see that one," I said. "I guess because it's the only house that isn't right on the street."

"The lights are on, and they've got a pumpkin in the window," Walker announced. "Let's check it out."

We trooped up to the front stoop and pushed the doorbell. The front door swung open instantly. A small, white-haired woman poked out her head. She squinted through thick eyeglasses at us.

"Trick or treat!" the four of us chanted.

"Oh my goodness!" she exclaimed. She pressed wrinkled hands against her cheeks. "What wonderful costumes!"

Huh? Wonderful costumes? I thought. *Two bedsheets and a borrowed Superman suit from last year?*

The old woman turned back into the house. "Forrest, come see this!" she called. "You've got to see these costumes."

I heard a man cough from somewhere deep inside the house.

"Come in. Please come in," the old woman pleaded. "I want my husband to see you." She stepped back to make room for us to enter.

The four of us hesitated.

"Come in!" she insisted. "Forrest has to see your costumes. But it's hard for him to get up. Please!"

Tabby led the way into the house. We stepped into a tiny, dimly lit living room. A fire blazed in a small brick fireplace against one wall. The room felt like a blast furnace. It had to be five hundred degrees in there!

The woman shut the front door behind us. "Forrest! Forrest!" she called. She turned to us and smiled. "He's in the back room. Follow me."

She opened the door and let us enter. To my surprise, the back room was enormous.

And jammed with kids in costumes.

"Whoa!" I cried out, startled. My eyes quickly swept the room.

Most of the kids had taken off their masks. Some of them were crying. Some were red-faced and angry. Several kids sat cross-legged on the floor, their expressions glum.

"What's going on?" Tabby demanded shrilly. Her eyes bulged wide with fear.

"What are they all doing here?" Lee asked, swallowing hard.

A red-faced little man with shaggy white hair came hobbling out from the corner, leaning on a white cane. "I like your costumes," he said, grinning at us.

"We—we have to go now," Tabby stammered.

We all turned to the door. The old woman had shut it behind her.

I glanced back at the kids in costumes. There were at least two dozen of them. They all looked so frightened and unhappy.

"We have to go," Tabby repeated shrilly.

"Yeah. Let us out of here," Lee insisted.

The old man smiled. The woman stepped up beside him. "You have to stay," she said. "We like to look at your costumes."

"You can't go," the man added, leaning heavily on his cane. "We have to look at your costumes."

"Huh? What are you *saying*? How long are you going to keep us here?" Tabby cried.

"Forever," the old couple replied in unison.

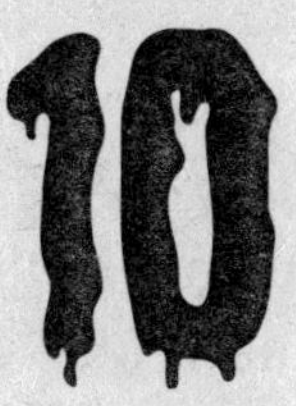

That was my daydream.

I was down by the street in front of my house, waiting for my friends to show up. And day-dreaming about Tabby and Lee being trapped by a weird old couple who liked to collect trick-or-treaters and keep them forever.

Of course, in my daydream, Walker and I sneaked out a side door.

But Tabby and Lee were caught before they could escape. And they were never seen again.

Nice daydream, huh?

I was still picturing the whole thing when Walker, Shane, and Shana finally arrived. And we eagerly trooped inside and up to my room.

"Drew, why are you grinning like that?" Shana demanded, dropping down onto the edge of my bed.

"I was just having a very funny daydream," I told her. "About Tabby and Lee."

"What could be funny about those two creeps?" Walker demanded. He picked up a tennis ball from the floor and tossed it to Shane. The two of them started tossing the ball back and forth across my room.

"It was very funny," I replied, sitting up and stretching. "Especially the ending."

I told them the whole daydream. I could see from the smiles on their faces that they enjoyed it.

But Shana scolded me. "We don't have time for daydreams, Drew. We need a real plan. It's almost Halloween."

Walker tossed the tennis ball too high. It smashed into my dresser lamp and knocked it over.

Shane hurtled toward the lamp and made a diving catch before it hit the floor.

"Way to go!" Walker cried. "Catch of the Month!" He slapped Shane a high five. He hit Shane so hard, the poor guy almost dropped the lamp.

"Grrrrrrr!" I growled at Walker and pointed to the desk chair. "Sit down. We have serious thinking to do."

"She's right," Shana agreed. "We have to scare Tabby and Lee out of their skins this year. We have to pay them back for the last two years. We *have* to!"

"So what are we going to do?" Walker demanded, dropping his long, lanky body into the desk chair. "Hide behind some bushes and yell 'Boo!'?"

Bad attitude.

"I've been thinking of some really scary things we could do at a party," I started. "I think—"

"No party!" Shana interrupted.

"Right. No party," her twin agreed. "We worked so hard on last year's party. And then Tabby and Lee didn't show up."

"Grrrrr." Just thinking about last year made me growl.

"Well, if we don't scare them at a Halloween party, where do we scare them?" Walker asked, tapping out a rhythm with his fingers on the desk.

"Shane and I have some really good ideas," Shana said.

"Yeah. I think you have to listen to Shana and me this year," Shane chimed in. "We have a really good plan. It will have them shaking for a year. Really!"

Walker pulled the desk chair closer. Shane sat on the floor beside him. I leaned closer to Shana on the bed.

Speaking in a low voice just above a whisper, Shana told Walker and me their plan. A very scary plan.

It gave me a chill just hearing Shana describe it.

"It's very simple," Shana finished. "Very easy to do. And there's no way it won't work."

"We'll give Tabby and Lee a Halloween they'll never forget!" Shane boasted.

"It's really mean," Walker murmured.

I gazed at the chubby, pink-cheeked twins. They were so cute-looking. So sweet and innocent. But their plan to frighten Tabby and Lee really was truly horrifying!

"It's mean," I agreed. "And it's cruel. And it's terribly gross and shocking." I grinned. "I *like* it!"

We all laughed.

"So we agree?" Shane asked. "We're doing it?"

We all agreed. We all solemnly shook hands.

"Great," Shana declared. "So Drew, all you have to do is invite them to come trick-or-treating with you. Shane and I will do the rest."

"No problem," I replied, still grinning. "No problem."

We all cheered and congratulated each other. We knew this was the year—*our* year.

Shana started to say something else—but my mom poked her head into the room.

"What are you four plotting so seriously?" Mom asked.

"Uh . . . nothing," Walker answered quickly.

"Just making plans for Halloween, Mom," I told her.

Mom bit her lower lip. Her expression turned serious. "You know, Drew," she said, shaking her head, "I don't think I can let you go trick-or-treating this year."

11

"Mom—you *have* to let me go trick-or-treating! You *have* to! Or else you'll spoil all of our plans for revenge!"

Those words *almost* burst from my mouth.

But somehow I held them in.

I choked back the words and stared hard at her, trying to decide if she was serious.

She was.

"Mom—what's wrong?" I finally cried. "What did I do? Why am I grounded?"

"Drew, you're not grounded." Mom laughed. "I just don't think trick-or-treating is a good idea this year. Haven't you seen the news stories? About the people in town who disappeared?"

"Huh? Disappeared?"

My mind flashed back to my daydream. I pictured the old couple again, locking kids up in their back room.

"You mean kids have disappeared?" I asked.

Mom shook her head. "No. Not kids. Adults. A fourth person was reported missing yesterday. Here. Look."

Mom had the newspaper rolled up under her arm. She pulled it out and unrolled it. She held the front page up so we all could see it.

I could read the bold, black headline from across the room:

LOCAL MYSTERY: 4 HAVE VANISHED

I climbed up from the bed and made my way over to Mom. I saw Shane and Shana exchange worried glances. Walker's expression had turned solemn. He drummed his fingers tensely on the desktop.

I took the newspaper from Mom and stared at the photos of the four people who had disappeared. Three men and one woman.

"The police are warning people to be very careful," Mom said softly.

Walker went over and took the newspaper from my hands. He studied the photos for a moment. "Hey—these people are all big!" he exclaimed.

Now we all clustered around the paper and stared at the gray photos. Walker was right. All four people were huge. The first one, a bald man in a bulging turtleneck sweater, had to be at least six foot six!

"Weird," I murmured.

Shane and Shana had grown strangely silent. I guessed they were frightened.

"Why would four large people just disappear?" Walker asked.

Mom sighed. "That's what the police would like to know," she said.

"But, Mom, if only adults are disappearing, why can't I go trick-or-treating?" I asked.

"Please let Drew go," Shana pleaded. "It's our last year to go out on Halloween night."

"No. I don't think so," Mom replied, biting her bottom lip again.

"But we'll be *really really really* careful!" I promised her.

"I don't think so," Mom repeated. "I don't think so."

Once again, Halloween was completely ruined.

But then Dad thought maybe trick-or-treating would be okay.

It was two days later. He and Mom had been discussing it nonstop.

"You can go out if you go in a group," Dad said. "Stay in the neighborhood. And don't wander away from the others. Okay, Elf?"

"Thanks, Dad!" I cried. I was so happy, I didn't remind him to stop calling me Elf! Instead, I surprised him with a big hug.

"Are you sure about this?" Mom asked.

"Of course he is!" I cried.

No way was I going to let them change their minds. I was already halfway to the phone to tell Walker that our plan was back on!

"There will be a thousand kids trick-or-treating in the neighborhood," Dad argued. "Besides, Drew and her friends are old enough and smart enough to keep out of trouble."

"Thanks, Dad!" I cried again.

Mom wanted to keep the discussion going. But I ran out of the kitchen and up to my room before she could get a word out.

I called Walker and told him the good news. He said he would call Shane and Shana and tell them to get ready for trick-or-treat night.

Everything was set. I had just one little problem left.

I had to convince Tabby and Lee that they should go trick-or-treating with us.

I took a deep breath and called Tabby's house. Her mother said she was over at Lee's, helping him get his Halloween costume ready.

So I hurried over to Lee's house. It was a gray Saturday afternoon. It had rained all morning, and the storm clouds still floated overhead.

The front lawns shimmered from the clinging rainwater. I jumped over wide puddles on the sidewalk. I wore a heavy gray sweatsuit. But the air felt damp and cold, and I wished I had put on a jacket over it.

I jogged the last block to Lee's house, partly to warm up. I stopped to catch my breath on the front stoop. Then I pushed the doorbell.

A few seconds later, Lee answered the door.

"Whoa!" I cried out when I saw his costume. He had bobbing antennas on his head. He wore a fuzzy yellow vest, pulled over a black-and-yellow-striped girl's swimsuit.

"You—you're a bee?" I stammered.

He nodded. "Tabby and I are still working on it. We bought black tights for my legs this morning."

"Cool," I said. He looked really stupid.

But why should I tell him?

Tabby greeted me as I stepped into the den. She had opened the package containing the tights and was stretching them out, tugging them hard between her hands.

"Drew—have you lost weight?" she asked.

"Excuse me? No."

"Oh. I guess you *like* your sweatsuit baggy like that—huh?"

She's so mean.

She turned her head away. But I saw her snicker to herself. She thinks she's really funny.

"Is that your costume?" she asked.

I decided to ignore her nasty jokes. "No. I'm going to be some kind of superhero, I think," I told her. "You know. Wear a cape and tights. What are you going to be?"

"A ballerina," she replied. She handed the tights to Lee. "Here are your bee legs. Do you have some heavy construction paper?"

"What for?" Lee asked.

"We need to make the stinger. You know. To glue to the back of your tights."

"No way!" Lee protested. "No stinger. I don't need a stinger. I'll only sit on it anyway."

I let them argue for a few minutes. I kept out of it.

Lee finally won. No stinger.

Tabby pouted for a while and made faces at him. She hates it when she doesn't get her way. But he's even more stubborn than she is.

"Listen, guys," I started. "Walker and Shane and Shana and I are all going to trick-or-treat together this year." I took a deep breath, then asked my question. "Want to come with us?"

"Yeah. Sure," Lee replied.

"Okay," Tabby agreed.

And that was that.

The trap was set.

Tabby and Lee were in for the most frightening Halloween of their lives.

Unfortunately, we were, too.

The week dragged by. I counted the hours till Halloween.

Finally, the big night arrived. I was so nervous, I could barely get my superhero costume together.

It wasn't much of a costume. I wore bright blue tights and a blue top. I pulled a pair of red boxer shorts over the tights.

For my cape, I cut up a red tablecloth we didn't use anymore and tied it around my shoulders. Then I pulled on a pair of white vinyl boots. I had a red cardboard mask that just covered my eyes.

"Super Drew!" I proclaimed to the mirror.

I knew the costume was lame. But I didn't care. Tonight wasn't about costumes. It was about terror. It was about scaring two kids to death!

I grabbed a large brown shopping bag from the closet to use as a trick-or-treat bag. Then I scrambled down the stairs, hoping to get out of the house before running into my parents. I hoped to avoid a last-minute lecture about how I had to be careful outside.

No such luck.

Dad stopped me at the bottom of the stairs. "Wow! Great costume, Elf!" he exclaimed. "What are you supposed to be?"

"Please don't call me Elf," I muttered. I tried to get past him to the front door, but he blocked my way.

"Just let me take one photo," he said.

"I'm kind of late," I told him. I was supposed to meet Walker on the corner at seven-thirty. It was already a quarter to eight.

"Be careful out there!" my mother called from the den.

Dad disappeared to get his camera. I waited at the bottom of the stairs, tapping my hand on the banister.

"Don't talk to any strangers!" Mom called.

Very helpful.

"Okay. One quick shot," Dad said, returning with his camera raised to his eye. "Stand against the door. You look great, Drew. Are you Wonder Woman or something?"

"Just a superhero," I mumbled. "I've really got to go, Dad."

He steadied the camera over his eye. "How about a smile?"

I gave him a toothy grin.

He clicked the shutter.

"Oh. Wait. Did it flash?" he asked. "I don't think I had the flash on." He examined the camera.

"Dad—" I started. I thought about Walker, standing by himself on the corner. Walker hated to wait. I knew how tense he'd be.

As tense as me.

"Dad, I've got to meet my friends."

"If you see anyone suspicious, run away!" Mom called from the den.

"Let's try again, Elf." Dad raised the camera again. "Smile."

He clicked the shutter. No flash.

"Whoa—" He checked the camera again.

"Dad, please—" I begged.

"Oh, wow," he murmured. "Would you believe it? The battery is dead." He shook his head. "I think I have an extra one upstairs. It will only take a second."

"Dad!" I screamed.

The doorbell rang. It startled us both.

"Probably some trick-or-treaters," Dad said.

I leaped to the door and pulled it open. I squinted into the yellow porch light. A boy stood there all in black. He wore a black sweater and black pants. A black wool ski cap was pulled down over his face. And he wore black gloves.

"Cute costume," Dad declared. "Get him a candy bar, Drew."

I groaned. "Dad, it's not a trick-or-treater.

It's Walker." I pushed open the storm door so that Walker could come in.

"I thought you were going to meet me," he said.

Dad stared at Walker's all-black costume. "What are you supposed to be?" he asked.

"A dark and stormy night," Walker replied.

"Huh? Where's the stormy part?" I asked.

"Here," Walker replied. He raised a black plastic water pistol and squirted me in the face.

Dad burst out laughing. He thought that was a riot. He called Mom in from the den to take a look.

"We're never getting out of here," I whispered to Walker. "We're going to miss Tabby and Lee."

We had the night all planned out, down to the minute. But now the whole plan could be ruined.

I had a knot in my stomach. I could feel it tightening. The cape suddenly felt as if it were choking me.

Mom and Dad were admiring Walker's costume. "A dark and stormy night! Very clever," Mom said. "But how will anyone see you in the dark? You'd better be very careful crossing the street."

Mom had advice for everyone tonight.

I couldn't take it anymore. "We've got to go. Bye," I said. I shoved Walker out the door and followed right behind him.

Mom called out more warnings from the house. But I couldn't hear her. I pulled Walker down the driveway, and we hurried toward the corner. That's where we were supposed to meet Tabby and Lee.

Our two victims.

"You should have stayed on the corner," I scolded Walker. "Maybe Tabby and Lee were here already and left."

"But you were so late," Walker protested. "I thought maybe something was wrong."

My heart was thumping. The knot in my stomach grew even tighter. "Okay, okay," I urged. "Let's just calm down."

It was a clear, cold night. A light frost made the lawns silvery. Overhead, a silver of moon rested near a cluster of bright stars.

Most of the houses on the block had their lights on. I saw two groups of little trick-or-treaters across the street. They were all hurrying up to the same house. A dog barked excitedly in the house next door.

I turned my eyes to the corner where we were supposed to meet Tabby and Lee. No one there.

Walker and I stopped under the street light. I adjusted my cape. It was really choking me. I saw that I hadn't cut it short enough. The bottom was soaked from dragging along the ground.

"Where are they?" I demanded.

"You know they're always late," Walker replied.

He was right. Tabby and Lee loved to keep people waiting for them.

"They will be here any second," Walker said.

A tall hedge ran along the corner yard. Walker started pacing back and forth from the hedge to the curb. His outfit was so black, when he stepped into the shadow of the hedge, he completely disappeared!

"Could you stop pacing—?" I started.

But my voice caught in my throat when I heard a cough. From the other side of the hedge.

A low, gruff cough.

Not a human cough. More like an animal growl.

I turned and saw that Walker had heard it, too. He stopped pacing and stared at the hedge.

I heard a scraping sound. The hedge appeared to shiver.

"Wh-who's back there?" I choked out.

The hedge shook again. Shook and cracked.

"Hey—who *is* it?" Walker cried.

Silence.

The hedge shook. Harder this time.

"Is this a joke or something?" Walker demanded in a trembling voice.

Another low animal growl.

"Noooo!" I cried out as two ugly creatures came snarling through the hedge.

I saw only a blur of ragged fur. Open jaws. Saliva-covered teeth.

Before I could move, one of the creatures leaped onto me, snarling and growling. It shoved me roughly down to the grass. And dug its fangs into my shoulder.

14

I let out a shrill wail of pain.

I tried to scramble to my feet. But the snarling creature had me pinned to the ground.

"Stop! *Stop!*" I struggled to squirm free as the creature tugged my cape over me, covering me like a blanket.

"Hey!" I heard Walker's angry shout. But I couldn't see what was happening to him.

"Noooooo! Let me go!" I shrieked.

With a frantic burst of energy, I reached up one hand—and swiped at the creature's drooling face.

To my shock, the whole face pulled off easily.

A mask. I held a rubber mask in my hand.

I stared up at a grinning face.

It took me a few moments to recognize the boy. Todd Jeffrey. Yes. Todd Jeffrey, the high-school kid who had frightened us all at Lee's party two years ago.

"Todd," I murmured. I frantically pulled the cape away from my face.

"Gotcha! Gotcha good!" he whispered. He let go of me and stood up.

"You creep!" I cried angrily. I tossed the rubber mask in his face.

He caught it in one hand and laughed. "Drew, can't you take a joke?"

"Huh? A joke? A *joke?*" I screamed.

I climbed to my feet and furiously began brushing myself off. My cape was totally tangled and covered with wet brown leaves.

Walker had been wrestling with the other creature. The guy pulled off his mask. Of course it was Joe, Todd's disgusting friend.

"Hope we didn't *scare* you!" he teased. He and Todd laughed like hyenas. They fell all over each other, slapping high fives and low fives.

Before I could tell them what jerks they were, I heard more laughter. To my surprise, Tabby and Lee came stepping out from behind the hedge. And all four of them enjoyed a good laugh together.

"Grrrrrrr!" I uttered a furious growl. At that moment, I wished I really *were* a superhero. I wanted to plow my superfists into their laughing faces.

Or maybe spread my cape and fly away—far away, so I wouldn't have to see any of them anymore.

"Happy Halloween, Drew!" Tabby called smugly.

"Happy Halloween!" Tabby and Lee repeated in unison, grinning their disgusting grins.

"How long were you and Lee standing back there?" I demanded angrily.

"Long enough!" Lee snickered. He and Tabby both burst out laughing again.

"We were standing back there the whole time," Tabby declared. "I *love* Halloween—don't you?"

I growled under my breath. But I didn't say anything.

Keep cool, Drew, I instructed myself. Tabby and Lee and their two high-school buddies played a little joke on you.

But they won't have the last laugh.

When the night is over, I told myself, *Walker and I will be the ones who are laughing.*

When Shane and Shana arrive, we are going to terrify them. Truly terrify them.

Todd and Joe had pulled their monster masks back on. They tilted back their heads and howled like wolves. Todd's mask was really gross. It had rubber saliva dripping over the long, pointy fangs.

"They're not coming trick-or-treating with us—are they?" I asked Tabby.

Tabby shook her head. She adjusted the tiara on top of her blond hair.

"No way!" Todd replied from behind the ugly mask. "Joe and I are too old to trick-or-treat. Especially with you crybabies."

"Then why are you wearing those monster costumes?" Walker demanded.

"Just to scare kids," Joe replied. He and Todd laughed again, loud, cruel laughs.

Joe grabbed my mask and pulled it down to my chin. Todd pulled the ski mask down over Walker's eyes. Then they ran off to find some other victims.

What creeps.

I was glad to see them go. I stood watching them, making sure the didn't change their minds and come back.

"Nice guys," Lee said. He set his orange and black trick-or-treat bag down on the grass. Then he adjusted his bee antennas.

I heard kids laughing across the street. I turned and saw a group of four kids—all monsters and goblins—running up the driveway to a house.

"Let's get going," Tabby said. "It's kind of cold."

"Aren't Shane and Shana supposed to meet us?" Lee asked.

"Yeah. They'll catch up to us," I said.

We crossed the street and started toward the first house, a tall, brightly lit brick house with a smiling pumpkin cutout in the front window.

As we made our way up the gravel driveway, I glanced at my watch.

And gasped.

Nearly eight-fifteen.

Shane and Shana were supposed to meet us on the corner at eight.

Where *were* they?

They were never late. Never.

I swallowed hard.

Was this Halloween about to be ruined, too?

Had something gone wrong?

We stepped up onto the front stoop and peered through the glass storm door. A big orange cat with bright blue eyes stared back at us from the other side of the door.

I rang the doorbell.

A few seconds later, a smiling young woman in jeans and a yellow turtleneck came hurrying to the door. She carried a basket of Snickers bars and Milky Ways.

"You all look great," she declared, dropping a candy bar in each bag.

"Drew—hold up your bag!" Tabby ordered shrilly.

"Oh. Sorry." I was still worrying about Shane and Shana. I held up my bag for the woman. The cat narrowed its amazing blue eyes at me.

"Are you supposed to be a princess?" the woman asked Tabby.

"No. A ballerina," Tabby replied.

"And you're a lump of coal?" the woman asked Walker.

"Something like that," Walker muttered. He didn't do his dark-and-stormy-night routine. I guessed he was worried about Shane and Shana, too.

"Have fun," the woman said. She pulled the storm door shut.

The four of us jumped off her stoop and started across the frost-covered grass to the next yard. When I glanced back to the door, I saw the cat still staring out at us.

The next house was dark. So we crossed the lawn to the house next door to it. A group of kids was already on the front stoop, shouting, "Trick or treat! Trick or treat!"

"Where *are* they?" I whispered to Walker.

He shrugged.

"If they don't show up . . ." I started. But I saw Tabby watching me. So I didn't finish my sentence.

We waited for the kids to leave, then climbed up to the stoop. Two little kids—probably three or four years old—were handing out little bags of candy corn to everyone.

They laughed at Lee's bee costume. They wanted to feel the antennas. The little boy asked Lee where his stinger was.

"I stuck it in someone," Lee told him.

They stared hard at Walker's all-black outfit.

I think it kind of frightened them. “Are you supposed to be a monster?” the little girl asked Walker timidly.

“No. I’m a lump of coal,” Walker told her.

She nodded seriously.

We hurried away and did three more houses to the end of the block. I saw two kids that I babysit for. They were in matching robot costumes. I stopped to talk with them for a minute.

Then I had to run to catch up to the others. They had crossed the street and had started doing the houses on the other side.

A strong gust of wind fluttered my cape. I shivered— and glanced nervously at my watch again.

Where were they? Where *were* Shane and Shana?

The whole plan depended on them. . . .

“Wow! Pretty good haul so far!” Lee declared. He held his bag open, studying the contents as we crossed the street.

“Did you get any Kit Kats?” Tabby demanded. “I’ll trade anyone for Kit Kats.”

“Only one person gave out apples,” Lee said, making a disgusted face. He reached into his bag and pulled out the apple. Then he heaved it as hard as he could across the yard.

The apple hit a tree trunk with a loud *thunk*. Then it bounced into the next driveway.

“Why do people give out apples?” Lee grumbled. “Don’t they know we only want candy?”

"Some people are just cheap," Tabby said. She pulled out her apple and dropped it in the grass. Then she kicked it with the toe of her ballet slipper.

They both really deserve what they're going to get, I thought. *They're both really jerks.*

But where are Shane and Shana?

We trick-or-treated our way down the block. It was getting pretty late, and there were fewer little kids out.

The streetlight near the corner was broken. We stepped into a patch of deep shadow.

One of Lee's antennas kept slipping off. He slid it back into place for the tenth time.

As we neared the corner, a tall tree blocked the moonlight, and it grew even darker.

"Oh—!" I let out a cry as two figures leaped out at us from behind the tree.

I thought that Todd and Joe had returned.

But I quickly saw that it wasn't those guys.

In a gray blur, the two figures turned their backs on us, blocking our way. They wore dark robes that flowed straight down to the ground. And over their heads . . .

Over their heads . . .

They wore pumpkins!

Large, round pumpkins, perfectly balanced on their shoulders.

"Whoa!" Walker let out a startled cry. He backed up and stumbled into me.

Tabby and Lee gaped in surprise.

But the most horrifying surprise was yet to come.

As they slowly turned to face us, their jack-o'-lantern faces came into view.

Eerie, jagged grins cut into their pumpkin heads.

Flashing triangle eyes.

Lit by flames!

Bright orange and yellow flames danced inside their heads!

And as the pumpkin heads turned their fiery, ragged grins on us, Walker and I opened our mouths and screamed in terror.

Our screams echoed down the block.

The fire flashed in the pumpkin heads' eyes.

I turned to Tabby and Lee. The light from the fiery jack-o'-lantern faces flickered over their faces. They stood calmly, staring at the grinning pumpkin heads.

Tabby turned to me. "Is this your idea of a joke? Were you trying to scare us?"

"We *know* it's Shane and Shana," Lee said. He tugged at one of the dark, loose, flowing costumes. "Hey, Shane—how's it going?"

The two pumpkin heads remained silent.

"How did you get the fire to work? Do you have candles in there?" Tabby demanded. "How can you see?"

The pumpkin heads grinned back in silence. A lick of fire darted out from one of the jagged mouths.

I shivered. These costumes were *too* good. I could hear the flames hiss inside the big orange heads. The costumes were dark green, like pumpkin vines.

Why aren't Tabby and Lee frightened? I wondered.

I expected Shane and Shana to appear in something frightening. But I didn't expect anything as good as these fiery jack-o'-lantern heads.

The costumes were great. But I felt so disappointed. Tabby and Lee were definitely not frightened.

This Halloween is going to be a disaster—like the others, I thought.

I stepped up beside Walker. I couldn't see his expression under his ski mask.

"How do they do the fire?" he whispered. "It's really awesome!"

I nodded. "But it didn't scare Tabby and Lee," I whispered back.

"It's early," Walker whispered. "Shane and Shana have just started."

My cape had become tangled around my legs. I tugged it free and tossed it behind me.

The two pumpkin heads still hadn't said a word.

Tabby picked up her trick-or-treat bag and turned to me. "You'll have to do better than this if you want to scare Lee and me," she said with a sneer.

"We're not scaredy-cats like you two," Lee boasted.

Flames darted out of the pumpkin heads' eyes. They both tilted their big heads as they stared at Tabby and Lee.

How do they do that? I wondered. *How do they control the flames? Do they have some kind of remote control?*

"Well, are we going to stand here and freeze? Or are we going to trick-or-treat?" Tabby demanded.

"Let's do *your* block," I suggested to her.

Tabby started to reply—but a hiss of fire from the nearest pumpkin head made her stop.

"*Let's go somewhere else,*" the jack-o'-lantern said from somewhere inside the pumpkin head. His voice came out in a hoarse crackle. Too harsh to be a whisper. A dry, choked sound.

"*Somewhere else,*" his partner echoed. Her voice also came out in a hoarse crackle. Like dry, dead leaves being crinkled together.

"Excuse me?" Lee cried.

"*We know a better neighborhood,*" the first pumpkin head crackled. The jagged mouth, cut through the thick pumpkin flesh, didn't move. The voice hissed from inside. The orange and yellow flames tossed in rhythm to the words.

"*We know a better neighborhood.*"

"*A neighborhood you won't forget.*"

Tabby laughed. She rolled her eyes. "Oh, wow. Scary voices!" she said sarcastically.

"Oooh, I'm shaking! I'm shaking!" Lee teased.

He and Tabby laughed together.

"Give us a break, guys," Tabby said to the pumpkin heads. "Your costumes are pretty good.

But they didn't scare us. So lose the creepy voices, okay?"

"Yeah," Lee agreed. "Let's go do some houses. It's getting late."

"*Follow ussss*," one of the pumpkin heads hissed.

"*Follow us to a new neighborhood. A better neighborhood.*"

They led the way down the street. Their big heads bounced on their shoulders as they walked. The fire flickered from their heads, casting a glow like lighted torches.

"What are they doing?" Walker whispered in my ear. "This isn't in the plan. Where are they taking us?"

I didn't know.

We walked three blocks, heading away from our houses. We passed a row of big stone houses set back on wide lawns behind tall hedges. The next block had an empty lot where someone had started to build a house, and then stopped.

The two pumpkin heads walked quickly, taking long strides. Their heads bounced on their shoulders. They kept their fiery faces straight ahead and didn't glance back at us.

"Where are we going?" Lee demanded, jogging to catch up to them. He tugged at one of their shoulders. "You're passing a lot of good houses across the street."

The jack-o'-lantern creature didn't slow down. "*Let's try a new neighborhood,*" he crackled.

"*Yessssss,*" his partner hissed. "*A new neighborhood. A better neighborhood. You'll see.*"

They led us past the empty lot. Past a row of small, dark houses.

"Where are we going?" Walker whispered. He

motioned to Shane and Shana. "What is their problem? Why are they doing this? They're starting to scare *me*!"

"I'm sure they know what they're doing," I whispered back.

I gazed around the block. I didn't see many other trick-or-treaters. It was getting late, and most of the little kids had already gone home.

In the next driveway, two tall kids—a gorilla and a chubby clown—were pawing through their trick-or-treat bags. They had their heads lowered to the bags. We passed by them, and they didn't even look up.

"Hey—we're missing a lot of good houses!" Lee protested. He pointed to a brick house on the corner. "Can we stop there? Those people always give out handfuls of candy bars. Really. Handfuls!"

The pumpkin heads ignored him and kept walking.

"Hey—whoa! Stop!" Tabby demanded.

She and Lee both trotted up in front of the pumpkin heads.

"Stop! Come on—whoa!"

"A new neighborhood," one of them croaked.

"Let's try a new neighborhood," the other one echoed.

"A better neighborhood."

A chill ran down my back. Shane and Shana were acting so *weird*.

I tugged my cape off a clump of weeds. The air suddenly felt colder, and damp. I wrapped the cape around me.

Up ahead, Lee fiddled with his bee antenna. I saw that Tabby's ballet slippers were soaked with mud.

We followed the pumpkin heads across the street. And then they stepped off the sidewalk and started into a dark woods.

Walker hurried up beside me. Even through his heavy makeup, I could see the worried expression on his face. "Why are they taking us into the woods?" he whispered.

I shrugged. "I guess they're getting ready to scare Tabby and Lee."

Twigs and dead leaves crackled under our shoes as we made our way between the trees.

A frightening thought flashed into my mind. I suddenly pictured the four people who had disappeared.

Four people. Vanished into thin air. Never seen again.

I remembered all of my mother's warnings. I remembered how she told us to stay where there were a lot of kids and a lot of bright lights.

I remembered how she didn't even want me to go trick-or-treating tonight.

This is wrong, I realized.

Mom's advice was smart. We shouldn't be walking through the woods tonight, I knew.

We shouldn't be away from the street, away from the brightly lit houses.

We shouldn't go off by ourselves like this in the dark, creepy woods.

"*A new neighborhood*," a pumpkin head crackled from up ahead.

"*Just past these woods*," the other one whispered. "*A really good neighborhood. You'll see.*"

The light from inside their heads flickered over the dark tangles of bare trees and tall weeds.

My heart began to thud. I hurried to keep up with the others.

Shane and Shana are good friends, I told myself.

I'm sure they know where they're going.

But this isn't what we planned. This isn't what we planned at all.

Why do I have such a bad feeling about this?

"Shane! Shana! Give us a break!" Tabby complained shrilly. "Look at me! Look at my ballerina skirt!"

She held up the front of the skirt. Even in the dim light, I could see the mud stain on the front.

"We have to get out of these woods!" Tabby wailed angrily.

"Yeah. It's too dark. And we're wasting too much time," Lee agreed.

His trick-or-treat bag got caught on a low tree limb. He tugged it hard to pull it loose.

Shane and Shana ignored the complaints. The big, fiery pumpkins bouncing on their shoulders, they made their way steadily and quickly through the darkness of the woods.

A few minutes later, we stepped out onto a narrow street. Seeing the bright street lights and rows of little houses, we all let out a happy cheer.

"*Now we can trick-or-treat,*" one of the pumpkin heads croaked.

I turned my eyes up and down the street. I saw house after house, all small, all on tiny lawns. Most of them had lights on in front. Many of them were decorated for Halloween.

The houses stretched for blocks. Two rows of brightly lit little houses—as far as I could see.

"This *is* an awesome neighborhood for trick-or-treating!" I declared, starting to feel a lot better. A lot less frightened.

"Excellent!" Lee agreed. "We'll clean up here!"

"Where are we?" Walker demanded. "How come I've never seen this neighborhood before?"

No one answered him. We were all too eager to get started.

I pulled some wet leaves off my cape and straightened my mask. Tromping through the woods had messed all of us up. We took a few seconds to get our costumes in better shape.

Then the six of us hurried up to the first house.

A young woman carrying a baby in one arm came to the door. She dropped miniature candy bars into our bags. The baby stared at the flaming pumpkin heads and smiled.

At the next house, an elderly couple took forever getting to the door. "Trick or treat!" we shouted at the top of our lungs. They raised their hands to their ears. I guess they couldn't stand the noise.

"I'm sorry. But we don't have any candy," the old woman said. She dropped nickels into our bags. A nickel per bag.

We hurried across the small yard to the next house. Two girls, about seven or eight, greeted us at the door. "Awesome costumes!" one of them said to Shane and Shana. They gave us little bags of M&M's.

"This is cool!" Lee declared as we hurried to the next house.

"The houses are so close together," Tabby added. "We can do a hundred houses in no time!"

"Why didn't we ever come here before?" Walker asked.

"Trick or treat!" we screamed as we rang the doorbell on the next house.

A teenaged boy with long blond hair and an earring in one ear answered the door. He snickered at our costumes. "Cool," he muttered. Then he dropped packages of candy corn into our bags.

On to the next house. And the next and the next.

We did the next block, stopping at every house. Then we covered two more blocks. The little houses seemed to stretch on forever.

My trick-or-treat bag was nearly full. We stopped at the corner because Walker's shoe had come untied. While he bent down to tie it, we all stopped to catch our breath.

"*Hurry up!*" a pumpkin urged Walker. Flames leaped angrily from his eyeholes.

"*Yesssss, hurry,*" the other one hissed. "*No time to wasssssste.*"

"Give me a break," Walker murmured. "I have a knot."

As he struggled with his shoe, the two pumpkin heads bobbed and squirmed impatiently.

Finally, Walker climbed to his feet and picked up his bulging trick-or-treat bag. The pumpkin heads were already leading the way to the next block of houses.

"I'm getting a little tired," I heard Lee whisper to Tabby. "What time is it?"

"My bag is nearly full," Tabby replied. With a groan, she shifted the heavy bag to her other hand.

"*Hurry,*" a pumpkin head insisted. "*Lots more houses to do.*"

"*Lotssssss,*" the other one hissed.

We did two more blocks. Both sides of the street. About twenty houses.

My bag was filled to the top. I had to carry it in both hands.

Walker's shoelace had come undone again. When he bent to tie it, it ripped in his hand. "*Now* what am I going to do?" he muttered.

"*Hurry,*" a pumpkin head insisted.

"*More houses.*"

"I'm getting tired," Tabby complained, loud enough for everyone to hear this time.

"Me, too," Lee agreed. "And this trick-or-treat bag is getting heavy."

“Stupid shoelace,” Walker muttered, still bent over his shoe.

“I guess it *is* getting pretty late,” I said, gazing around. “I don’t see any other trick-or-treaters. I think they’ve all gone home.”

I pulled off my cape. It was all tangled, and it was starting to choke me. I balled it up and tucked it under my arm.

“*More houses*,” one of the pumpkin heads whispered.

“*Hurry. Lots more to do*,” the other one insisted in her dry, crackling voice. The yellow flames danced inside her head.

“But we want to quit!” Lee whined.

“Yes. We’re done,” Tabby agreed shrilly.

“*You can’t quit!*” a pumpkin head snapped.

“Huh?” Lee’s mouth dropped open.

“*Keep going! You can’t quit!*” the pumpkin head insisted.

They both appeared to float up, to rise up over us. The fires raged in their triangle eyes. The heads floated up over the dark, caped bodies.

“*You can’t quit! You can’t EVER quit!*”

19

"Ha-ha. Very funny." Tabby rolled her eyes.

But I saw Lee step back in fear. His knees seemed to buckle, and he nearly dropped his trick-or-treat bag.

"*Another block,*" a pumpkin head insisted.

"*Another block. And then another.*"

"Whoa. Wait a minute!" Tabby protested. "You can't boss us around like that. I'm going home."

She turned and started to walk away. But the two pumpkin heads moved quickly to block her path.

"Let me go!" Tabby protested.

She darted sharply to the right. But the big pumpkin creatures floated with her. Their fiery grins appeared to grow wider. Brighter.

The two of them began circling us, floating silently. They swirled around us, faster and faster—until it looked as if we were surrounded by flames.

A wall of leaping flames all around us!

"*You will obey!*" came the crackling command.

The flames pushed us from behind. Forced us forward.

We had no choice but to obey them. We were prisoners. Prisoners of their fire.

An old man was standing at the door to the first house. He grinned at us as we stepped onto his front stoop. "You kids are out kind of late—aren't you?" he asked.

"Kind of," I replied.

He dropped candy bars into our bags.

"*Hurry,*" a pumpkin head urged as we crossed the wet grass to the next house. "*Hurry!*"

Lee's trick-or-treat bag was so heavy, he dragged it along the ground. I carried mine in both hands. Tabby complained to herself, muttering and shaking her head.

We did both sides of the block. I didn't see any other kids out. No cars came by. Some of the houses were turning out their lights.

"*Hurry!*" a pumpkin head insisted.

"*Lots more houses. Lots more blocks.*"

"No way!" Lee cried.

"No way!" Tabby repeated. She tried to sound strong. But I heard a tremble in her voice.

The jack-o'-lantern faces loomed over us once again. The fiery eyes stared out at us.

"*Hurry. You can't stop now! You CAN'T!*"

"But it's too late!" I protested.

"And my shoe keeps coming off," Walker chimed in.

"We don't want to trick-or-treat anymore," Tabby told them shrilly.

"You can't stop now! Hurry!"

"Lots more houses. This is the BEST neighborhood!"

"No way!" Tabby and Lee repeated together. They started to chant. "No way! No way! No way!"

"Our bags are full," I said.

"Mine is starting to tear," Walker complained.

"No way! No way!" Tabby and Lee chanted.

The two jack-o'-lanterns began to swirl around us again, circling faster and faster, rebuilding the wall of flames. *"You mussssst not sssssstop!"* one of them hissed.

"You musssst keep going!"

They swirled closer. So close I could feel the scorching heat of their flames.

And as they swirled, they began to hiss, like snakes about to strike.

The hissing grew louder, louder—until it sounded as if we were *surrounded* by snakes!

My heavy trick-or-treat bag fell from my hands. "Stop!" I screamed up at them. "Stop it! You're not Shane and Shana!"

Fire leaped from their eyes. Their hisses became a high wail.

"You're not Shane and Shana!" I shrieked. "Who are you?"

20

They swirled to a stop. Bright flames licked out of their grinning mouths. Their shrill wails bounced off the bare trees, cutting through the heavy night silence.

"Who are you?" I demanded again, my voice trembling. My whole body shook. I suddenly felt as if the cold of the night had seeped inside me.

"Who are you? Have you done something to our friends?"

No reply.

I turned to Walker. The light of the flames flickered over his face. Through his black makeup, I could see his frightened expression.

I swallowed hard and turned to Tabby and Lee. They were both sneering and shaking their heads.

"Is this your idea of a dumb Halloween joke?" Tabby demanded. She rolled her eyes. "Wow. Did you really think Lee and I would fall for this?"

"Ooh—I'm scared! I'm scared!" Lee cried sarcastically. He made his knees knock together. "Look—I'm shaking like a leaf!"

He and Tabby let out loud laughs.

"These are real clever costumes. Great fire effects. But we know it's Shane and Shana," Lee declared. "No way you're going to scare us, Drew."

"No way," Tabby repeated. "Look!"

She and Lee reached out their hands. They each grabbed a pumpkin head—and tugged.

"Whoa!"

They pulled the fiery pumpkin heads off the creatures' shoulders.

And then all four of us screamed—because the two costumed figures *had no heads underneath*!

Our screams rose up shrilly, cutting through the night air like wailing sirens.

The pumpkin head fell from Tabby's hand and bounced heavily on the ground. Bright orange flames shot out of its eyes and mouth.

Lee still gripped the other pumpkin head between his hands. But he dropped it when the jagged mouth began to move.

The fiery heads grinned up at us from the grass.

"Ohhh." I uttered a low moan of terror and staggered back. I wanted to run away, to run as fast as I could and not look back.

But I couldn't take my eyes off the two heads, grinning up at us from the wet grass.

As I stared, my heart pounded and my legs began to shake. Someone grabbed my arm.

"Walker!"

He held on to me. His hand was as cold as ice. With his other hand, he pointed to the two headless bodies.

They stood in their dark, flowing costumes. They hadn't moved. The spot between their shoulders where their heads had rested was flat and smooth.

As if the pumpkin heads had been balanced there. But never attached.

Never attached.

Tabby and Lee huddled together beside me. Tabby's tiara was missing. Her hair had come unpinned. It fell in wet tangles over her face.

Lee's trick-or-treat bag had toppled onto its side. A pile of candy had spilled over the grass, inches away from one of the pumpkin heads.

The flames inside the heads danced and flickered. And then the jagged mouths began to move.

The smiles grew wider. The triangle eyes narrowed.

"Hee hee hee heeeeee."

An ugly laugh escaped their mouths. An evil, dry sound. More like a throat clearing, more like a cough than a laugh.

"Hee hee heeeeeeeee."

"Noooo!" I moaned. Beside me, I heard Walker gasp.

Lee swallowed hard. Tabby was holding on to the sleeve of his bee costume with both hands. She pulled him back until they were standing behind Walker and me.

"Hee hee heeeeeeeee."

The heads laughed together, flames flickering inside them.

Their two bodies moved quickly. They reached out long arms and grabbed the heads up from the grass.

I expected them to place the heads back on their shoulders. But they didn't. They held the heads in front of their chests.

"*Hee hee heeeeeee.*"

Another dry laugh. The pumpkin mouths twisted on the dark, round faces. The eyes stared blankly at us, bright orange, then shadowy, flickering with the flames.

I realized I was squeezing Walker's arm. He didn't even seem to notice.

I let go. And took a deep breath.

"Who are you?" I called to the two creatures. My voice came out high and tiny. "Who are you? And what do you want?"

"*Hee heee heeeee.*" They laughed their ugly laughs again.

"Who are you?" I choked out again, shouting over their dry, crackling laughter. "Where are Shane and Shana? Where are our friends?"

Flames hissed from the two heads. Their ragged orange grins grew wider.

"Drew—let's try one more time to run away," Walker whispered. "Maybe if we catch them by surprise . . ."

We both spun around and started to run. Tabby and Lee came stumbling after us.

My legs felt so wobbly and weak, I didn't think I could run. My heart pounded so hard, I struggled to breathe.

"Run!" Walker cried breathlessly, pulling my arm. "Drew—faster!"

We didn't get far.

Uttering their shrill, frightening hisses, the creatures whirled around us once again. Trapping us. Holding us prisoner inside their circle of flames.

No way we could run away. No way we could escape from them.

Peering over the flying flames, I searched desperately up and down the street.

No one in sight. Nothing moved. No cars. No people. Not even a dog or a cat.

Holding their heads at their waists, the two creatures stepped up to us. They stood over us menacingly, raising the red, glowing heads high above their bare shoulders.

"More houses. More houses." The jack-o'-lantern lips pushed out the words. The red eyes stared down at us.

"More houses. More houses."

"You cannot stop. You must keep on trick-or-treating!"

"Pick up your bags. Pick them up—now!" one of them growled. Her head held up between two hands, she gazed down at us, her jagged lips forming an evil sneer.

"We—we don't *want* to trick-or-treat!" Lee wailed, holding onto Tabby.

"We want to go home!" Tabby cried.

"More houses. More houses. More houses." The pumpkin heads continued their hissing chant.

They bumped us together. They bumped and pushed us.

We had no choice. Wearily, we picked up our trick-or-treat bags from where they had fallen on the grass.

They moved behind us, chanting, chanting in their low, dry whispers. *"More houses. More houses."*

They pushed us to the first house on the block. They pushed us onto the front stoop. Then they hovered close behind.

"How—how long do we have to trick-or-treat?" Tabby demanded.

The pumpkin heads grinned together. *"Forever!"* they declared.

A woman came to the door and dropped packages of Hershey's kisses into our bags. "You kids are out awfully late," she said. "Do you live around here?"

"No," I replied. "We don't really know where we are. We're in a strange neighborhood, and we're being forced to trick-or-treat by two headless pumpkin creatures. And they say they're going to make us trick-or-treat forever. Help us—please! You've got to help us!"

"Ha-ha! That's good!" the woman laughed. "That's very funny. You have a very good imagination." She closed the door before I could get out another word.

At the next house, we didn't even bother to ask for help. We knew no one would believe us.

"Your bags are so full!" the woman exclaimed. "You must have been trick-or-treating for hours!"

"We . . . we like candy a lot," Walker replied wearily.

I glanced back at the pumpkin heads. They were motioning impatiently. They wanted us to move on to the next house.

We said good-bye to the woman and made our way across the front yard. Our trick-or-treat bags were heavy, so we dragged them along the grass.

As we headed to the next driveway, Tabby hurried up beside me. "What are we going to do?" she whispered in my ear. "How are we going to get away from these . . . these *monsters*?"

I shrugged. I didn't know how to answer her.

"I'm so scared," Tabby confessed. "You don't think these pumpkin creatures really plan to make us trick-or-treat *forever*—do you? What do they really want? Why are they doing this to us?"

"I don't know," I said, swallowing hard. I could see that Tabby was about to cry.

Lee was walking with his head down. He dragged his bulging trick-or-treat bag behind him. He was shaking his head, muttering to himself.

We stepped up to the next porch and rang the bell. A middle-aged man in bright yellow pajamas opened the door. "Trick or treat!" we cried wearily.

He dropped little Tootsie Rolls into our bags. "Very late," he muttered. "Do your parents know you're still out?"

We dragged on to the next house. And the next.

I kept waiting for a chance to escape. But the two creatures never let us out of their sight. They stayed right with us, keeping in the shadows. Their eyes glowed red from the deepening fire inside their heads.

"More houses," they chanted, forcing us to cross the street and do the long row of houses on the other side.

"More houses."

"I'm so scared," Tabby repeated to me in a trembling whisper. "So is Lee. We're so scared, we feel sick."

I started to tell her I felt the same way.

But we both gasped when we saw someone walking along the street.

A man in a blue uniform!

At first I thought he was a policeman. But as he stepped under a streetlight, I saw that he wore a blue work uniform. He had a blue baseball cap on his head. He carried a large black lunch box in one hand.

He must be coming home from work, I told myself. He was whistling softly to himself, walking with his head down. I don't think he saw us.

Tabby changed that. "Helllllp!" she screamed. "Sir—please! Help us!"

The man raised his head, startled. He squinted at us.

Tabby began running across the grass to him. The rest of us followed, dragging our heavy trick-or-treat bags.

"Help us—please!" Tabby pleaded shrilly. "You've got to save us!"

The four of us hurtled breathlessly into the street. We surrounded the startled man. He narrowed his eyes at us and scratched his brown, curly hair.

"What's wrong, kids? Are you lost?" he asked.

"Monsters!" Lee exploded. "Headless jack-o'-lantern monsters! They've captured us! They're forcing us to trick-or-treat!"

The man started to laugh.

"No—it's true!" Tabby insisted. "You've got to believe us! You've got to help us!"

"Hurry!" Lee cried.

The man scratched his hair again. He squinted at us hard, studying our faces.

"Hurry! Please hurry!" Lee wailed.

I stared back at the startled man.

Would he help us?

"You've *got* to help us!" Lee pleaded.

"Okay. I'll go along with the joke," the man said, rolling his eyes. "Where are your monsters?"

"There!" I cried.

We all turned back to the front yard.

No one there. The pumpkin heads were gone.

Disappeared.

Tabby gasped. Lee's mouth dropped open.

"Where did they go?" Walker murmured.

"They were standing right there!" Tabby insisted. "Both of them. Holding their heads in their hands! Really!"

The man let out a long sigh. "You kids have a good Halloween," he said wearily. "But give me a break, okay? I just got off work, and I'm beat."

He shifted his black lunch box to the other hand. Then we watched him make his way up the driveway. He disappeared around the back of the house.

"Let's get *out* of here!" Lee cried.

But before we could run, the two pumpkin heads leaped out from behind a low hedge. The red flames hissed inside their heads. Their jagged mouths were turned down in angry snarls.

"More houses," they insisted, rasping the words together. *"More houses. You can't stop trick-or-treating."*

"But we're so tired!" Tabby protested. Her voice cracked. Again, I saw tears wetting her eyes.

"Let us go—please!" Lee begged.

"More houses. More!"

"You can never stop! NEVER!"

"I can't!" Lee cried. "My bag is full. Look!" He held out the bulging trick-or-treat bag to the pumpkin heads. Candy bars spilled over the top.

"Mine is full, too!" Walker declared. "It's filled to the top. I can't squeeze another piece of candy corn in it!"

"We have to go home!" Tabby cried. "Our bags are totally full."

"That's no problem," one of the pumpkin heads replied.

"No problem?" Tabby wailed. "No problem?"

"Start eating," the pumpkin head ordered.

"Huh?" We all gasped.

"Start eating," he insisted. *"Start eating."*

"Hey—no way!" Lee protested. "We're not going to stand here and—"

The creatures appeared to rise up. Bright yellow flames shot out from their eyes. A roar of hot wind escaped their jagged, snarling mouths. The wind burned my face.

We all knew what would happen if we refused to do as they said. We'd end up inside the flames.

Lee grabbed a chocolate bar from the top of his trick-or-treat bag. He tore off the wrapper with a trembling hand. And he shoved the candy into his mouth.

We all started to eat candy. We had no choice.

I shoved a Hershey bar into my mouth and started to chew. I couldn't even taste it. A big gob stuck to my teeth. But I shoved in more and kept chewing.

"Faster! Faster!" the pumpkin heads ordered.

"Please!" Tabby begged, with a mouthful of red licorice. "We can't—"

"Faster! Eat! Eat!"

I shoved an entire bag of candy corn into my mouth and struggled to chew. I saw Walker pawing through his bag, looking for something he could eat quickly.

"Faster! Eat!" the fiery heads demanded, floating over us. *"Eat! Eat!"*

Lee choked down his fourth 3 Musketeers bar. He grabbed a Milky Way and started to unwrap it.

"I—I'm going to be sick!" Tabby declared.

"Faster! Faster!" came the raspy command.

"No. Really. I feel sick!" she cried.

"Eat more! Eat—faster!"

Lee started to choke. A gob of pink taffy shot out of his mouth. Tabby slapped him on the back until he stopped coughing.

"More! Faster!" the pumpkin heads ordered.

"I—I can't!" Lee cried in a hoarse whisper.

The creatures leaned over him, angry flames shooting from their eyes.

Lee grabbed a Crunch bar, tore off the wrapper, and bit into it.

All four of us huddled there on the curb, gobbling down candy. Chewing as fast as we could. Forcing it down, then shoving in some more.

Trembling. Frightened. Feeling sick.

We had no idea that the biggest horror was still to come.

25

"I . . . can't . . . eat . . . any more," Tabby choked out.

We had been stuffing ourselves with candy for several minutes. Tabby had chocolate running down her chin. And I saw chocolate stuck in the tangles of her blond hair.

Lee was bent over on the grass. He held his stomach and groaned. "I don't feel so hot," he murmured. He let out a long, loud burp. And groaned again.

"I never want to see another candy bar in my life," Walker whispered to me.

I tried to reply. But my mouth was full.

"More houses!" one of the pumpkin heads ordered.

"More houses! More trick-or-treating!"

"No—please!" Tabby begged.

Bent over on the grass, Lee let out another long burp.

"It's almost midnight!" Tabby protested. "We have to go home!"

"There are many houses to go," a pumpkin head told her, narrowing its fiery eyes. *"Houses forever. Trick-or-treat forever!"*

"But we feel sick!" Lee moaned, holding his stomach. "We can't do any more houses tonight!"

"Everyone has gone to sleep," Walker told the pumpkin heads. "No one will answer the door this late."

"They WILL in this neighborhood!" the pumpkin head replied.

"No problem in THIS neighborhood," the other creature agreed. *"In this neighborhood, you can trick-or-treat FOREVER!"*

"But—but—but—" I sputtered.

I knew it was no use. The fiery creatures were going to force us to keep going. They weren't going to listen to our complaints.

And they weren't going to let us go home.

"More houses! More! Trick-or-treat forever!"

Tabby helped Lee to his feet. She picked up his trick-or-treat bag and placed it in his hand. Then she brushed her hair out of her face and picked up her own bag.

The four of us trooped across the street, dragging the bags beside us. The night air had grown cold and heavy. A strong breeze rattled the trees and sent brown leaves scuttling past our feet.

"Our parents must be so worried," Lee murmured. "It's really late."

"They *should* be worried!" Tabby declared in a trembling voice. "We may never see them again."

The porch light at the first house was still on. The pumpkin heads forced us onto the porch.

"It's too late to trick-or-treat," Lee protested.

But we had no choice. I rang the bell.

We waited. Shivering. Feeling heavy and sick from all the candy we had forced down.

Slowly, the front door opened.

And we all gasped in shock.

"Ohhh!" A low cry escaped Walker's throat.

Lee jumped off the porch.

I stared at the creature in the yellow porch light. A woman. A woman with a grinning jack-o'-lantern head.

"Trick or treat?" she asked, turning her jagged smile on us. Orange flames danced and flickered inside her head.

"Uh—uh—uh—" Walker hopped off the porch and stumbled into Lee.

I stared at the grinning pumpkin head. *This is a nightmare!* I told myself. *A living nightmare!*

The woman dropped some kind of candy into my bag. I didn't even see what it was. I couldn't take my eyes off her pumpkin head.

"Are you—?" I started to ask.

But she closed the front door before I could get the words out.

"More houses!" the pumpkin heads commanded. *"More trick-or-treating!"*

We dragged ourselves to the next little house. The door swung open as we climbed onto the front stoop.

And we stared at *another* pumpkin-head creature.

This one wore jeans and a maroon sweatshirt. The flames hissed and crackled behind his eyes and mouth. Two wide, crooked teeth were carved into his mouth—one on top, one below—giving him a silly expression.

But my friends and I were too terrified to laugh.

At the next house, we were greeted by two jack-o'-lantern creatures. We crossed the street and found another fiery-headed creature waiting for us at the next house.

Where are *we?* I wondered.

What is *this strange neighborhood?*

The two pumpkin heads forced us on to the next block. The houses here all had jack-o'-lantern creatures living in them.

At the end of the block, Tabby set down her trick-or-treat bag and turned to face the pumpkin heads. "Please—let us stop!" she begged. "Please!"

"We can't do any more houses!" Lee exclaimed weakly. "I—I'm so tired. And I really feel sick."

"Please—?" Walker pleaded. "Please—?"

"I can't do another house. I really can't," Tabby said, shaking her head. "I'm so frightened. Those creatures . . . in every house . . ." She uttered a sob and her voice trailed off.

Lee crossed his arms over the front of his striped costume. "I'm not taking another step," he insisted. "I don't care what you do. I'm not moving."

"Me neither," Tabby agreed, stepping close beside him.

The two pumpkin heads didn't reply. Instead, they rose up high in the air.

I took a step back as their triangle eyes bulged wide and their mouths stretched open. Bright orange flames flew from their eyes.

And then their mouths stretched even wider. And they both let out high wails. The shrill sound rose and fell through the heavy night air. Rose and fell, like police sirens.

The pumpkin heads tilted back until their flames shot straight up to the sky. And their siren wails grew louder. Louder. Until I had to hold my hands over my ears.

I saw a flash of light. And turned to see another pumpkin head floating toward us from across the street.

"Oh!" I uttered a hoarse cry as two more pumpkin-head creatures hurried out of their houses.

And then two more. And another creature. And another.

All down the block, doors flew open.

Creatures floated out. Floated toward us. Hissing and wailing.

Flickering, dancing flames shot out from their jack-o'-lantern eyes and mouths, sending orange light into the black sky. They floated and bobbed down the street, across the dark lawns, wailing like sirens, hissing like snakes.

Closer. Closer.

Dozens of them. Dozens and dozens.

Walker, Tabby, Lee, and I pressed close together in the middle of the street as the pumpkin-head creatures drew near.

They formed a circle around us. A circle of grinning, fiery jack-o'-lantern faces over dark-robed bodies.

The circle of creatures spun around us slowly. And as they spun, their heads bobbed and tilted on their shoulders.

Slowly, slowly, they spun around us. And then they began to chant in their hoarse, crackly voices:

"*Trick or treat! Trick or treat! Trick or treat!*"

"What do they want?" Tabby cried. "What are they going to do?"

I didn't have a chance to answer her.

Four creatures stepped quickly into the middle of the circle.

And when I saw what they carried in their hands, I started to scream.

27

"Trick or treat! Trick or treat! Trick or treat!"

My scream drowned out the chanting pumpkin heads.

And as the four creatures stepped forward, the chanting stopped. Their jack-o'-lantern heads bobbed on their shoulders. Their ragged smiles grew wider as they came near.

They held their hands waist high. In their hands, they each held a pumpkin head.

Four extra pumpkin heads!

"Oh, no!" Lee cried out when he saw them.

Tabby grabbed Lee's arm in terror. "What are they going to do with those heads?"

Bright yellow flames flickered from the eyes and grinning mouths of the four extra heads.

"*These are for you!*" a pumpkin head announced in a voice that sounded like sharp pieces of gravel being rubbed together.

"Ohhh!" A low moan escaped my throat.

I stared at the empty heads, stared at their fiery eyes, their ugly grins.

"These are for you," the pumpkin head repeated, stepping closer. *"These will be your new heads!"*

"No! You can't! You *can't*!" Tabby screamed. "You—"

Her cry was cut off as one of the creatures raised a pumpkin head over her. It had a hole cut in the bottom. The creature slammed the pumpkin head over Tabby's head.

Lee tried to run.

But a creature moved quickly to block his way—and then slammed a pumpkin head onto Lee's head.

I stumbled back, my mouth open in amazement.

Hands pressed helplessly against the sides of their pumpkin heads, Tabby and Lee ran down the street. Ran blindly. Ran screaming. Screaming into the darkness.

And then the creatures turned to Walker and me. And raised the empty pumpkin heads high.

"Please!" I begged. "Please—no!"

"Please!" I cried. "Please don't give me a pumpkin head!"

"Please—" Walker joined in.

And then we both burst out laughing.

The two creatures set the empty pumpkin heads down on the ground. And then their own pumpkin heads started to change. The flames died out. The heads began to shrink. And change shape.

A few seconds later, Shane and Shana had their own heads back.

And then all four of us started to laugh. We hugged each other and spun around. We danced wildly, crazily, up and down the street. We tossed back our heads and laughed at the moon and stars. Laughed till it hurt.

"It worked, guys!" I exclaimed when we finally stopped celebrating. "It worked! It worked! We really scared Tabby and Lee this time!"

"They'll be scared for the rest of their lives!" Walker declared. He slapped Shane on the back.

Then he danced another happy dance, waving his hands gleefully above his head.

"We did it! We did it!" I chanted joyfully. "We really scared them! We finally scared them!"

"That was so much fun!" Walker exclaimed. "And so easy!"

I stepped up to Shane and Shana and hugged them both. "Of course," I exclaimed, "it helps to have two aliens from another planet as friends!"

"Whoa! Take it easy!" Shane warned, lowering his voice. He glanced around nervously.

"We don't want any strangers to know that we're not from Earth," Shana said.

"I know, I know!" I replied. "That's why we didn't use your weird powers to scare Tabby and Lee before."

"This year, we were desperate!" Walker declared.

"But we've got to be very careful," Shana said.

Shane rose up and turned to all the other pumpkin-head creatures who still circled us. "Thanks for your help, brothers and sisters!" Shane called to them. "You'd better hurry home before anyone sees that we have invaded this whole neighborhood!"

Waving and laughing, murmuring happily to each other, the other pumpkin heads hurried back to their houses. In a few seconds, the street stood empty again—except for us four friends.

We started walking down the middle of the street, making our way home. Walker and I dragged our heavy trick-or-treat bags beside us.

Walker turned to Shane and Shana. A smile spread over his face. "When do you think Tabby and Lee will discover they can just pull off their pumpkin heads?" Walker asked.

"Maybe never!" Shana replied.

And we all started laughing all over again.

We didn't stop until we reached the bottom of my driveway.

"Thanks again," I told Shane and Shana. "You guys were great."

"You were greater than great! You were awesome!" Walker declared. "A couple of times, you even scared *me*! And I knew it was you!"

"And do you know what else is great about having aliens from another planet as friends?" I said. "You two don't eat candy."

"That's right," Shane and Shana agreed.

"That means Walker and I get to keep it all!" I exclaimed, laughing.

I suddenly had a serious thought. I stopped laughing. "You know, I've never *seen* you two eat," I told the two aliens. "What *do* you eat?"

Shana reached out and pinched my arm. "You're still really bony, Drew," she replied. "You'll find out what Shane and I eat when you fill out a bit."

"Yeah," Shane chimed in. "People from our planet only like to eat very large adults. So you don't have to worry for now."

My mouth dropped open. "Hey—you're kidding, right?" I demanded. "Shane? Shana? You're not serious—right? That's a joke. Right? *Right*?"

Want more chills?

Check out

THE HEADLESS GHOST

Here's a sneak peek!

1

Stephanie Alpert and I haunt our neighborhood.

We got the idea last Halloween.

There are a lot of kids in our neighborhood, and we like to haunt them and give them a little scare.

Sometimes we sneak out late at night in masks and stare into kids' windows. Sometimes we leave rubber hands and rubber fingers on windowsills. Sometimes we hide disgusting things in mailboxes.

Sometimes Stephanie and I duck down behind bushes or trees and make the most frightening sounds — animal howls and ghostly moans. Stephanie can do a terrifying werewolf howl. And I can toss back my head and shriek loud enough to shake the leaves on the trees.

We keep almost all the kids on our block pretty frightened.

In the mornings, we catch them peeking out their doors, seeing if it's safe to come out. And at night, most of them are afraid to leave their houses alone.

Stephanie and I are really proud of that.

During the day we are just Stephanie Alpert and Duane Comack, two normal twelve-year-olds. But at night, we become the Twin Terrors of Wheeler Falls.

No one knows. No one.

Look at us, and you see two sixth graders at Wheeler Middle School. Both of us have brown eyes and brown hair. Both of us are tall and thin. Stephanie is a few inches taller because she has higher hair.

Some people see us hanging out together and think we're brother and sister. But we're not. We don't have any brothers and sisters, and we don't mind one bit.

We live across the street from one another. We walk to school together in the morning. We usually trade lunches, even though our parents both pack us peanut-butter-and-jelly sandwiches.

We're normal. Totally normal.

Except for our secret late-night hobby.

How did we become the Twin Terrors? Well, it's sort of a long story. . . .

Last Halloween was a cool, clear night. A full moon floated over the bare trees.

I was standing outside Stephanie's front window in my scary Grim Reaper costume. I stood up on tiptoes, trying to peek inside to check out her costume.

"Hey—beat it, Duane! No looking!" she shouted through the closed window. Then she pulled down the shade.

"I wasn't looking. I was just stretching!" I shouted back.

I was eager to see what Stephanie was going to be. Every Halloween, she comes up with something awesome. The year before, she came waddling out inside a huge ball of green toilet paper. You guessed it. She was an iceberg lettuce.

But this year I thought maybe I had her beat.

I'd worked really hard on my Grim Reaper costume. I wore high platform shoes—so high that I'd tower over Stephanie. My black, hooded cape swung along the ground. I hid my curly brown hair under a tight rubber skullcap. And I smeared my face with sick-looking makeup, the color you see on moldy bread.

My dad didn't want to look at me. He said I turned his stomach.

A success!

I couldn't wait to make Stephanie sick! I banged my Grim Reaper sickle on Stephanie's window. "Hey, Steph—hurry up!" I called. "I'm getting hungry. I want candy!"

I waited and waited. I started pacing back and forth across her front lawn, my long cape sweeping over the grass and dead leaves.

"Hey! Where are you?" I called again.

No Stephanie.

With an impatient groan, I turned back to the house.

And a huge, hairy animal jumped me from behind and chewed off my head.

Well, it didn't *really* chew off my head.

But it tried to.

It growled and tried to sink its gleaming fangs into my throat.

I staggered back. The creature looked like an enormous black cat, covered in thick, black bristles. Gobs of yellow goo poured from its hairy ears and black nose. Its long, pointed fangs glowed in the dark.

The creature snarled again and shot out a hairy paw. "Candy . . . give me all your candy!"

"Stephanie—?" I choked out. It *was* Stephanie. Wasn't it?

The creature jabbed its claws into my stomach in reply. That's when I recognized Stephanie's Mickey Mouse watch on its hairy wrist.

"Wow. Stephanie, you look awesome! You really—" I didn't finish. Stephanie ducked behind the hedge and yanked me down beside her.

My knees hit the sidewalk hard. "Ow! Are you crazy?" I shrieked. "What's the big idea?"

A group of little kids in costumes paraded by. Stephanie leapt out of the hedge. "Arrrggghhh!" she growled.

The little kids totally freaked. They turned and started to run. Three of them dropped their trick-or-treat bags. Stephanie scooped up the bags. "Yummmm!"

"Whoa! You really scared them," I said, watching the little kids run up the street. "That was cool."

Stephanie started to laugh. She has a high, silly laugh that always starts me laughing, too. It sounds like a chicken being tickled. "That was kind of fun," she replied. "More fun than trick-or-treating."

So we spent the rest of the night scaring kids.

We didn't get much candy. But we had a great time.

"I wish we could do this every night!" I exclaimed as we walked home.

"We can," Stephanie said, grinning. "It doesn't have to be Halloween to scare kids, Duane. Get my meaning?"

I got her meaning.

She tossed back her bristly head and let out her chicken laugh. And I laughed, too.

And that's how Stephanie and I started haunting our neighborhood. Late at night, the Twin

Terrors strike, up and down our neighborhood. We're *everywhere*!

Well . . . *almost* everywhere.

There's one place in our neighborhood that even Stephanie and I are afraid of.

It's an old stone house on the next block. It's called Hill House. I guess that's because it sits up on a high hill on Hill Street.

I know. I know. A lot of towns have a haunted house.

But Hill House really is haunted.

Stephanie and I know that for sure.

Because that's where we met the Headless Ghost.

Hill House is the biggest tourist attraction in Wheeler Falls. Actually, it's the *only* one.

Maybe you've heard of Hill House. It's written up in a lot of books.

Tour guides in creepy black uniforms give the Hill House tour every hour. The guides will act real scary and tell frightening stories about the house. Some of the ghost stories give me cold shivers.

Stephanie and I love to take the tour—especially with Otto. Otto is our favorite guide.

Otto is big and bald and scary-looking. He has tiny black eyes that seem to stare right through you. And he has a booming voice that comes from deep inside his huge chest.

Sometimes when Otto leads us from room to room in the old house, he lowers his voice to a whisper. He talks so low, we can barely hear him. Then his tiny eyes will bulge. He'll point—and *scream*: "There's the ghost! There!"

Stephanie and I always scream.

Even Otto's smile is scary.

Stephanie and I have taken the Hill House tour so often, we could probably be tour guides. We know all the creepy old rooms. All the places where ghosts have been spotted.

Real ghosts!

It's the kind of place we love.

Do you want to know the story of Hill House? Well, here's the story that Otto, Edna, and the other guides tell:

Hill House is two hundred years old. And it's been haunted practically from the day the stones were gathered to build it.

A young sea captain built the house for his new bride. But the day the big house was finished, the captain was called out to sea.

His young wife moved into the huge house all alone. It was cold and dark, and the rooms and hallways seemed to stretch on forever.

For months and months, she stared out of their bedroom window. The window that faced the river. Waiting patiently for the captain's return.

Winter passed. Then spring, then summer.

But he never came back.

The captain was lost at sea.

One year after the sea captain disappeared, a ghost appeared in the halls of Hill House. The ghost of the young sea captain. He had come back from the dead, back to find his wife.

Every night he floated through the long, twisting halls. He carried a lantern and called out his wife's name. "Annabel! Annabel!"

But Annabel never answered.

In her grief, she had fled from the old house. She never wanted to see it again.

Another family had moved in. As the years passed, many people heard the ghost's nightly calls. "Annabel! Annabel!" Through the twisting halls and cold rooms of the house.

"Annabel! Annabel!"

People heard the sad, frightening calls. But no one ever saw the ghost.

Then, one hundred years ago, a family named Craw bought the house. The Craws had a thirteen-year-old boy named Andrew.

Andrew was a nasty, mean-natured boy. He delighted in playing cruel tricks on the servants. He scared them out of their wits.

He once threw a cat out of a window. He was disappointed when it survived.

Even Andrew's own parents couldn't stand to spend time with the mean-tempered boy. He spent his days on his own, exploring the old mansion, looking for trouble he could get into.

One day he discovered a room he had never explored before. He pushed open the heavy wooden door. It let out a loud creak.

Then he stepped inside.

A lantern glowed dimly on a small table. The boy saw no other furniture in the large room. No one at the table.

"How strange," he thought. "Why should I find a burning lantern in an empty room?"

Andrew approached the lantern. As he leaned down to lower the wick, the ghost appeared.

The sea captain!

Over the years, the ghost had grown into an old and terrifying creature. He had long, white fingernails that curled in spirals. Cracked, black teeth poked out from between swollen, dry lips. And a scraggly white beard hid the ghost's face from view.

The boy stared in horror. "Who—who are you?" he stammered.

The ghost didn't utter a word. He floated in the yellow lantern light, glaring hard at the boy.

"Who are you? What do you want? Why are you here?" the boy demanded.

When the ghost still didn't reply, Andrew turned—and tried to run.

But before he moved two steps, he felt the ghost's cold breath on his neck.

Andrew grabbed for the door. But the old ghost swirled around him, swirled darkly, a swirl of black smoke in the dim yellow light.

"No! Stop!" the boy screamed. "Let me go!"

The ghost's mouth gaped open, revealing a bottomless black hole. Finally, it spoke—in a whisper that sounded like the scratch of dead leaves. "Now that you have seen me, you cannot leave."

"No!" The boy shrieked. "Let me go! Let me go!"

The ghost ignored the boy's cries. He repeated his dry, cold words: "Now that you have seen me, you cannot leave."

The old ghost raised his hands to the boy's head. His icy fingers spread over Andrew's face. The hands tightened. Tightened.

Do you know what happened next?

4

The ghost pulled off the boy's head—and hid it somewhere in the house!

After hiding the head, hiding it away in the huge, dark mansion, the ghost of the sea captain let out a final howl that made the heavy stone walls tremble.

The terrifying howl ended with the cry, "Annabel! Annabel!"

Then the old ghost disappeared forever.

But Hill House was not freed from ghosts. A new ghost now haunted the endless, twisting halls.

From then on, Andrew haunted Hill House. Every night the ghost of the poor boy searched the halls and rooms, looking for his missing head.

All through the house, say Otto and the other tour guides, you can hear the footsteps of the Headless Ghost, searching, always searching.

And each room of the house now has a terrifying story of its own.

Are the stories true?

About the Author

R.L. Stine's books are read all over the world. So far, his books have sold more than 300 million copies, making him one of the most popular children's authors in history. Besides Goosebumps, R.L. Stine has written the teen series Fear Street and the funny series Rotten School, as well as the Mostly Ghostly series, The Nightmare Room series, and the two-book thriller *Dangerous Girls*. R.L. Stine lives in New York with his wife, Jane, and Minnie, his King Charles spaniel. You can learn more about him at RLStine.com.

R. L. Stine's Fright Fest!
Now with Splat Stats and More!
Goosebumps
The Werewolf of Fever Swamp
R.L. Stine
Goosebumps
A Night in Terror Tower
R.L. Stine
Goosebumps
Welcome to Dead House
R.L. Stine
Goosebumps
Welcome to Camp Nightmare
R.L. Stine
Goosebumps
Ghost Beach
R.L. Stine
Goosebumps
The Scarecrow Walks at Midnight
R.L. Stine
Goosebumps
You Can't Scare Me!
R.L. Stine
Goosebumps
Return of the Mummy
R.L. Stine
Goosebumps
Revenge of the Lawn Gnomes
R.L. Stine
Goosebumps
Phantom of the Auditorium
R.L. Stine
Goosebumps
Vampire Breath
R.L. Stine
Goosebumps
Stay Out of the Basement
R.L. Stine
SCHOLASTIC
Read them all!

Catch the MOST WANTED Goosebumps® villains UNDEAD OR ALIVE!

PLANET OF THE LAWN GNOMES

FRANKENSTEIN'S DOG

A NIGHTMARE ON CLOWN STREET

SPECIAL EDITIONS

SCHOLASTIC

scholastic.com/goosebumps

Goosebumps HorrorLand™
Goosebumps HorrorLand
REVENGE OF THE LIVING DUMMY
R.L. STINE
CREEP FROM THE DEEP
R.L. STINE
MONSTER BLOOD FOR BREAKFAST!
R.L. STINE
THE SCREAM OF THE HAUNTED MASK
R.L. STINE
DR. MANIAC VS. ROBBY SCHWARTZ
R.L. STINE
WHO'S YOUR MUMMY?
R.L. STINE
MY FRIENDS CALL ME MONSTER
R.L. STINE
SAY CHEESE – AND DIE SCREAMING!
R.L. STINE
WELCOME TO CAMP SLITHER
R.L. STINE

THE SCARIEST PLACE ON EARTH!

SCHOLASTIC

www.scholastic.com/goosebumps

GBHL19H2